AGAIN, A KISS GOODBYE

AGAIN, A KISS GOODBYE

TIMOTHY T. WULF

JJ OF RENO, INC.

CONTENTS

Prologue ... 1

Midwest Roots ... 7

The Man in the Airplane ... 13

Into the Sky ... 19

Responsibilities ... 27

The Path Forward ... 35

Georgia Tech Summer at Sea ... 45

The Dance of the Marksman ... 51

Unplanned Love ... 59

So Many Questions ... 67

Wings to the Future ... 75

Wings in Training ... 81

Wings of Their Own ... 87

A Mother's Intuition ... 95

Learning to Land ... 103

While America Begins to Awake ... 111

Delivering Buffalos ... 117

A Bump on the Head ... 127

Overboard ... 135

Becoming a W.A.S.P ... 143

Ace ... 149

Life in the Cockpit ... 157

Reunited in Paradise ... 163

Return to the Flame ... 171

The Weave ... 179

The Destroyer ... 185

The Triangle Island Run ... 193

Worth Saving ... 199

Trading in My Plane 211
Rotating Home 219
At Long Last 229
Epilogue 246

DEDICATION

To my father, Harold N. "Harry" Wulf, who learned to fly at the end of World War II and captained a B-25 Billy Mitchell bomber. His inspiring stories of flight helped spark my lifelong fascination with this chapter of history.

And to Paul Thayer—a great American aviator, World War II Navy fighter ace, test pilot, corporate leader, and cherished friend. His vivid recollections of wartime service in the Pacific were a gift to all who heard them, and a lasting influence on me.

PROLOGUE

Coral Sea – May 4, 1942

The sky shattered without warning.

Tracer fire ripped past Teddy's Wildcat, green arcs slicing the blue like thrown knives. The cockpit vibrated violently as his aircraft lurched, the engine howling in protest. He shoved the stick left, then right, feeling the plane respond sluggishly—too sluggish—and knew instantly he'd waited half a second too long.

A Zero flashed across his nose, so close Teddy caught the red sun on its wing and the dark shape of the pilot's helmet beneath the canopy. He squeezed the trigger out of reflex—

Nothing.

No chatter. No recoil. Just dead weight beneath his fingers and the hollow realization that his guns had jammed.

"Damn it," he muttered, voice lost beneath the engine's roar.

He pushed the Wildcat into a dive, trading altitude for speed, but the Zero stayed with him effortlessly, graceful and deadly. Teddy felt the impact before he heard it—a brutal hammer blow to the rear fuselage. The aircraft shuddered violently. Instruments danced. Another burst followed, sharper this time, metal tearing like cloth.

Warning lights bloomed.

Oil pressure—dropping.

RPM—unsteady.

The engine coughed.

"Easy... easy," Teddy whispered, one hand steady on the stick as the other swept across failing gauges. Another Zero streaked past above him, banking hard, the pilot already confident this fight was over.

But Teddy refused to give him the ending he wanted.

He yanked the throttle and hauled the Wildcat into a climbing turn no Zero pilot would expect from a wounded American fighter. The maneuver crushed him into his seat, vision narrowing, but it bought him space—just enough.

The carrier appeared ahead, impossibly small, a gray sliver in an endless ocean.

Home.

Flak burst nearby, black blossoms erupting in the air. The Zero broke away at the last moment, unwilling to follow him into the carrier's protective fire.

Teddy didn't celebrate.

The engine was dying.

Smoke streamed from the cowling now, thick and

oily. The Wildcat shook violently as he lined up his approach, hands slick with sweat inside his gloves. The deck rose and fell beneath him, pitching on the swell. Deck crew scattered, some pointing, some running.

"Landing gear—down," he said aloud.

The left wheel locked into place.

The right hesitated.

"No—come on—"

The deck rushed up.

The tailhook caught the wire with a savage snap, wrenching him forward in his harness. For half a heartbeat, he thought he'd made it.

Then the right wheel collapsed.

The Wildcat lurched violently to starboard. Sparks exploded as the wingtip slammed into the deck. The aircraft spun, momentum carrying it sideways in a shriek of tearing metal and fire.

Teddy had just enough time to think, this is going to hurt.

The plane slammed into the carrier's island. His right wing sheared off on impact. The cockpit filled with noise, light, and crushing force. His helmet struck the canopy frame—

And the world went white.

The blow came without pain.

Just light—white, absolute—then nothing at all.

When sensation returned, it did so cautiously.

Stillness first.

Then weight.

Teddy felt the solid press of a wooden chair beneath

him. His boots rested flat on a floor that did not move. Air touched his face without force, without urgency. No vibration. No engine. No screaming wind.

The smell was wrong.

Not oil.

Not smoke.

Dust.

Old paper.

Something faintly sweet—polish, maybe, or chalk.

Light filtered in slowly, warm and steady, angled rather than glaring. It fell across his hands, which were folded on a desk scarred with years of small cuts and initials. The surface was familiar beneath his palms in a way the cockpit never had been.

Sound returned next.

Muted.

Civilian.

A room breathing quietly around him.

Pages turning.

A chair shifting.

The distant hum of a world unconcerned with altitude or enemy fire.

His heartbeat slowed.

The tightness in his chest eased.

Whatever had been chasing him—whatever had been tearing at metal and sky—was gone now, already slipping beyond reach.

Teddy sat still, suspended in the moment just before awareness fully claimed him, the last echoes of flight fading as the ordinary pressed gently in.

He was no longer airborne.

He was somewhere safe.

Somewhere earlier.

And when he finally lifted his eyes, the classroom was already waiting.

By 1935, Hitler had risen to power in Germany and had denounced the World War I Versailles Treaty. He was in the process of expanding naval and army units, and murmurs of war were discussed around the world. In Japan, Japan had denounced naval treaties that it had with Britain and the United States, and they too were aggressively investing in their military. In the meantime, the United States and European allies had very little appetite for war, in that they had just previously ended World War I.

Theodore "Teddy" Davidson gazed out the tall classroom window as if the Kansas wind might carry him straight into the wide green fields beyond. Newly sprouted wheat shimmered under the April sun, stretching flat toward the horizon as tractors crawled through distant rows. A pair of coyotes trotted along a fence line, barely visible except for the flick of their tails. Out here, even the smallest movements felt like a story.

MIDWEST ROOTS

Livingston, Kansas - Spring 1936

Inside Room 104 of Livingston High School, however, it was junior English, and Mr. Wilson was taking roll.

"Peter?"

"Here."

"Mike?"

"Present."

"Teddy."

Silence.

"Theodore Davidson?" Mr. Wilson said, lifting an eyebrow.

Teddy blinked back into the moment. "Yes, sir. Sorry."

A few students chuckled. Teddy didn't mind. His mind lived half in the classroom, half beyond the horizon.

Tonight was the big game—Livingston versus Wamego—and scouts were rumored to be watching. As starting shortstop and two-time All-State player, Teddy thrived under pressure. He wasn't big, but he was quick, smart, and fearless. Baseball was instinct. He could read a stance, anticipate a pitch, or stretch a single into a double before most players reacted.

Yet the truth was, baseball wasn't everything. When he wasn't on the diamond, he lost himself in Popular Mechanics magazines, studying diagrams of engines and early aviation designs. He dreamed of leaving Kansas, studying engineering, building aircraft—maybe even flying them.

But for now, the bell rang, and life returned to familiar rhythms.

That evening, the Friday night lights glowed warm against the early spring air. The Livingston stands were full—neighbors wrapped in jackets, hands hugging paper cups of coffee as the sun slipped behind the bleachers. Teddy stepped onto the diamond, glove under his arm, heartbeat steady.

He played one of his finest games.

Three hits. Clean fielding. A sharp double that cleared the bases and broke the game open. When he jogged off the field, dust on his cleats and sweat on his brow, he felt entirely himself—confident, unburdened, alive.

Baseball brought clarity. The world made sense there.

The next afternoon, Livingston's annual Fireman's Festival brightened the town square. Farmers in overalls wandered the booths, mothers chased sticky-fingered children, and teenagers gathered under strings of bulbs hung from telephone poles. For Teddy, the music and chatter felt like home.

He drifted toward the shooting gallery, drawn by the metallic clatter of tin ducks racing along their rails. He placed a nickel on the counter and lifted the battered .22 rifle.

Five ducks fell in five shots.

Then ten.

Then twenty.

A crowd gathered.

The vendor squinted. "Say, kid, you planning to win my whole inventory?"

Teddy grinned. "Just warming up."

People laughed, but the moment meant more to him than anyone knew. His father had taught him to shoot in the back pasture—tin cans tossed skyward, sunlight in his eyes, the world holding still as he learned to trust both instinct and timing. Shooting wasn't performance—it was understanding motion, wind, and trajectory.

The same things, one day, an aviator might need.

He returned home that evening feeling full of life, warmed by the sounds and laughter of his small Kansas town.

But the house was quiet.

Unnaturally quiet.

A folded note lay on the kitchen table, held down by his mother's apron. Teddy lifted it and read the hurried lines:

There was an accident. Your father was hurt at the Mitchell farm. A steer kicked. His leg is badly injured. He's at the hospital.

For a long moment, Teddy stood perfectly still. The ticking of the wall clock grew louder than it had ever sounded. His father—the strongest, steadiest man he knew—injured and helpless? It felt impossible.

He didn't sleep that night.

By morning, Teddy was at the window when he saw the dusty green pickup turning down the lane. The truck bounced over the ruts, sun glinting off the hood. His heart pounded as he ran outside.

Before the vehicle fully stopped, Teddy pulled open the passenger door and climbed in.

"How's Dad?" he asked.

His mother looked older than she had yesterday—her shoulders tight, her hands trembling faintly on the wheel.

"He's not good, son," she said softly. "The damage is extensive. They're worried about infection. They don't know if they can save the leg."

The words hit him like a stone. Teddy stared through the windshield as farmland blurred past them.

"They don't know how long he'll be in the hospital," she continued, trying to steady her voice. "We'll need to take care of things here. All of it."

Teddy nodded slowly. The responsibility felt enormous—but clear.

Back home, the silence pressed in. He touched his father's hat on the peg by the door. The coffee mug still on the counter. The empty chair at the kitchen table. Ordinary things suddenly felt weighty, as if the house itself were holding its breath.

Outside, the wide Kansas fields bent gently in the morning wind, steady as ever. His father had worked this land his whole life. And now it needed him.

School, baseball, dreams of studying engineering— they all faded into the background.

Teddy Davidson straightened his shoulders.

He knew exactly what had to happen.

The farm needed him.

His mother needed him.

And he had never run from hard things.

Not once.

In 1930, the Dust Bowl had ravaged Midwestern farmers. The combination of drought and wind dramatically decreased the productivity of the land. Farmers were all suffering with low crop prices, with many farmers failing. One program the United States government introduced was the planting of wind roads along all roads in the Midwest, encouraging farmers to block the wind through trees. This program, although successful in the long run, was very slow, of course, to have any real impact on the agricultural status in 1935.

THE MAN IN THE AIRPLANE

The low hum reached Teddy before he even stepped out of the barn. It vibrated through the rafters, rattling dust on the beams and stirring something restless in his chest. He froze mid-swing with the pitchfork, head tilted. That engine sound—steady, rhythmic, impatient—was nothing like any tractor or truck he knew.

It was an airplane. And it was close. Very close.

He dropped the pitchfork and hurried into the sunlight. A warm Kansas breeze swept across the yard, carrying the scent of hay, earth, and something unfamiliar—oil and upper-air chill. He shaded his eyes.

A biplane descended over the eastern tree line in a graceful arc, sunlight glinting off its twin wings. Teddy recognized it instantly. He had seen that crop duster many times in the distance—dusting the Kellers' fields and others farther east—but his parents had never hired him. Their small acreage didn't require it.

But today, the biplane was coming in low. Very low.

The aircraft dipped, aligned with the open field beside the barn, and touched down in a rising cloud of dust. The propeller slowed, coughing once before settling. A lean, sun-hardened man stepped out, boots scuffed from countless landings, a grin bold enough to claim the whole county.

He strode toward Teddy.

"Son," the man said, extending his hand, "I'm Mark Sheraton. I'm the crop duster around here."

Teddy shook his hand, gaze drifting back to the plane—closer now, larger, louder, more alive than he had ever imagined.

"And I was there," Mark added, "when you hit five out of five ducks at the Fireman's Festival. Clean shots. That's rare talent."

Teddy felt his face warm with pride. "Thank you, sir."

Mark hooked his thumbs in his belt. "State's paying a bounty on coyotes. Ranchers are losing calves, and they're desperate. That got me thinking." He nodded toward the biplane. "How'd you like to try hitting a coyote from up there?"

Teddy blinked. "From the air?"

"Sure. You've got the aim. I've got the wings. Seems like the perfect partnership."

Teddy's mind raced. "Well... that'd take one heck of a shot."

"That's what makes it worth doin'. Now, the bounty is two dollars a hide. I can give you twenty-five cents apiece after fuel and upkeep."

Teddy straightened. "Well, sir... ammunition's not

free. I'd need fifty cents."

Mark burst into laughter. "You bargain like a rancher. All right—fifty cents it is. If you can hit 'em."

He reached into the cockpit and returned with a long white silk scarf—the kind aviators wore in magazines.

"Every real flyer wears one," Mark said, wrapping it around Teddy's neck. "Keeps the wind off. Makes you part of the sky."

Teddy touched the silk, breath catching. "Thank you, sir."

"Get your rifle," Mark said. "Let's take her up."

Teddy sprinted toward the house, scarf tails fluttering behind him. He burst into the kitchen.

His mother stood at the stove, flipping bacon in a cast-iron skillet, the room warm with the scent of breakfast. His father sat at the table, unable to rise because of his injured leg, but alert the moment he saw Teddy's face.

"What's all the rush?" his mother asked.

"Ma! Pa! I'm going up in a plane!" Teddy said breathlessly. "Mr. Sheraton—he landed right out back. He wants me to help hunt coyotes from the air!"

His father tried to stand. His hands gripped the table; his wounded leg trembled. Pain tightened his jaw, preventing him from rising. "A plane?" he asked, breathing hard. "That's what I heard settlin' out there?"

"Yes, sir!"

His mother turned sharply. "Teddy, you can't just—"

But his father raised a firm hand. "Mary. Let him be." He looked at Teddy, eyes filled with pride and worry. "Go on, son. You've dreamed of flyin' your whole life."

His mother's resistance faded into quiet fear. She wiped her hands on her apron. "Be careful. Please."

"I will," Teddy promised.

He grabbed his rifle and raced outside. His father, still gripping the table for balance, watched him from the kitchen doorway, frustration and pride warring in his expression.

Mark was already strapped into the front seat when Teddy arrived. "Climb into the second seat and hold on!"

Teddy climbed up, heart hammering, scarf streaming in the wind.

Inside the kitchen, his father leaned forward in his chair, straining to see out the window. His wife moved to his side, resting a gentle hand on his shoulder as they both watched the young biplane roll forward.

"I wish I could get out there," he muttered.

"I know," she whispered, her eyes never leaving their son.

Outside, the engine roared. The propeller blurred. Dust swirled.

The biplane surged forward, faster, faster—

And Teddy Davidson left the earth for the first time.

In 1937, the global political landscape grew even more volatile. Germany and Japan formally signed the Anti-Comintern Pact, marking the strengthening of what would later be known as the Axis Powers. Germany and Italy, meanwhile, lent political recognition to General Francisco Franco's government in Spain, having already contributed material and air support during the Spanish Civil War—most notably through the infamous German Condor Legion.

While Europe simmered with ideological conflict, Japan continued its aggressive expansion in the Pacific, asserting military dominance in China and threatening nearby territories. The United States, increasingly wary of Japanese ambitions, took early steps to restrict Japan's access to vital natural resources—especially oil and metals—foreshadowing greater tensions to come.

INTO THE SKY

The world dropped away so quickly that Teddy's breath caught in his throat. One moment the biplane was rattling across the field in a storm of dust and wind, and the next the wheels lifted—lightly, almost shyly—before the aircraft surged upward with a confidence that made Teddy's heart leap into his mouth.

He gripped the sides of the second seat, knuckles white, scarf snapping behind him like a white banner cutting through the morning air. The force of the climb pushed him back into the leather cushion. Wind tore at his hair, stung his eyes, and roared past his ears in a wild chorus.

But none of that mattered.

He was flying.

The earth folded beneath him like a quilt, stitched with fence lines, hedgerows, and thin dirt roads carving across their small corner of Kansas. He could see the Davidson farmhouse shrinking, then the barn, then the scattering of oaks by the creek. The entire farm compressed into something small, almost soft—like a memory he could hold in his hand.

Ahead, Mark Sheraton sat upright in the front seat, goggles on, cap pulled tight, his shoulders relaxed in a way that told Teddy he'd done this a thousand times and felt as natural in the air as he did on the ground.

Mark twisted slightly and shouted over the roar of the wind, "You holdin' on back there, Teddy?"

Teddy's answer was snatched away instantly, but Mark must have seen the enormous grin plastered across his face, because he gave a thumbs-up and laughed into the slipstream.

They continued climbing, the engine bellowing steadily, pulling them higher until the horizon stretched in an endless arc. The air grew cooler. The wind steadied. Teddy felt his pulse easing into the rhythm of the aircraft itself—as if his heart had found a new tempo in the sky.

The biplane leveled off.

Mark lifted his goggles briefly, wiped dust from his cheek with the back of his hand, and called back, "Not bad for your first takeoff!"

Teddy shouted, "It's incredible!"

Mark patted the fuselage affectionately. "She's a good

girl. Reliable as an old mule, but she climbs like she's got places to be."

Teddy couldn't argue. The aircraft felt alive, straining joyfully against gravity, eager to race across the wide open heavens.

They descended slightly into a slow sweep over the neighboring farms. The biplane moved with purpose, like a hawk surveying the land below.

"You ever been higher than a hayloft?" Mark teased.

"No, sir!" Teddy yelled. "Never been off the ground at all!"

"Well, son, today's your day."

They banked left, the wings tilting. Teddy's stomach lifted, but not unpleasantly—more like the drop of a roller coaster he'd ridden once at the county fair. The sort of movement that made him feel like his insides were laughing.

Mark pointed ahead. "We'll start sweepin' the creek beds. Coyotes like to sun themselves this time of day."

Teddy nodded, clutching the rifle across his lap.

The first few minutes were quiet except for the engine's steady drumming. Teddy's eyes scanned the ground with a hunter's instinct—every movement, every shadow catching his attention.

Mark banked gently. "We're lookin' for a flash of movement. Anything that don't belong. You see somethin', holler."

"Yes, sir!" Teddy called.

A sudden gust buffeted the wings, rattling the struts. Teddy jolted.

"Is that normal?" he asked, the words carried away on the wind.

Mark held the control stick with calm ease. "Perfectly normal! Air's like a river—got currents, pockets, eddies. She'll talk to you if you pay attention." He tapped the fuselage. "She's talkin' now. Nothin' to worry about."

Teddy forced himself to breathe.

Then—movement.

At first, just a flicker. A shape that didn't match the shadows.

"There!" he shouted. "By the bend! Two of 'em!"

Mark gave a sharp nod and banked the plane left. "Good eyes, boy! Keep watchin'!"

The biplane circled, angling lower as Mark controlled the throttle. The wind changed pitch. Teddy felt the aircraft sink slightly, then steady itself as Mark lined up the pass.

Teddy's heart hammered. The coyotes were visible now—two specks lying in the grass, lounging in the sun like they owned the world.

"Not yet!" Mark warned. "Let me bring you in close."

The air rushed faster now. The ground grew larger. Teddy could almost smell the dry grass baking in the heat.

"Now!" Mark shouted.

Teddy lifted the rifle.

The motion nearly ripped it from his hands—the wind was stronger than he expected. He tightened his grip, pressed the stock hard against his shoulder, and sighted the coyote nearest the creek.

Exhale.

Don't think.

Fire.

The shot cracked through the sky with a violent snap.

Dust flew behind the fleeing coyotes, who darted into the brush like streaks of lightning.

"I missed!" Teddy called, frustrated.

Mark threw his head back and laughed. "Missed? You nearly shaved that critter's backside! That's a damn fine shot for your first."

Teddy flushed but couldn't help smiling. "Let's go again!"

"That's the spirit!"

They circled around. Teddy steadied himself more quickly this time, adjusting for the vibration and the unpredictable pull of the wind. He angled the rifle lower, anticipating the sway of the biplane.

The coyotes had slowed now, confused by the noise and wind.

"Take the lead one!" Mark yelled.

Teddy inhaled, aimed, fired.

The bullet struck a patch of dirt directly in front of the coyote, scattering dust into its face. It yelped and darted away.

"So damn close!" Mark hollered. "Another few inches and he'd be on our tally!"

Teddy's grin widened. The disappointment faded quickly into excitement. He was improving—he could feel it. The sky was becoming something he could read, like a second language.

They climbed again, leveling out.

Mark glanced back. "How you feelin'?"

"Like I never want to come down!"

"Good! That's the feeling that keeps a pilot goin'." Mark chuckled. "Second only to not crashin'."

Another gust shook the biplane. Teddy braced himself, but this time he didn't panic. His body had begun adapting to the rhythm of the aircraft—the rise and fall, the sway and tilt.

They continued scanning the land. A few more coyotes appeared, and Teddy took shots—one landing so close it kicked dirt into a fleeing coyote's eyes.

"Closest yet!" Mark hollered. "You're a natural."

Teddy felt laughter bubbling out of him—real, free, unstoppable. He had never known anything like this.

Not plowing.

Not hunting deer.

Not watching planes from the ground.

This was different.

This was... destiny.

Mark must have sensed something, because he called back, "Feels right, don't it?"

Teddy nodded, the wind carrying away his voice.

"Some folks," Mark continued, "are born with their boots on the ground. Others... well..." He tapped the control stick. "Others are meant to rise."

Teddy swallowed against the lump forming in his throat.

They flew a wide arc back toward the Davidson farm. The barn grew visible first, then the farmhouse, then the thin line of smoke rising from the kitchen chimney.

Mark slowed the engine, adjusted the throttle, and lined up the field.

"Bringin' her home," he called. "Nice and easy."

The biplane dropped lower, wheels inches above the earth. They touched down in a swift, bouncing trot, skidding across the dirt before rolling to a steady crawl.

Dust enveloped them.

Teddy exhaled shakily.

Mark powered down the engine, and silence slowly replaced the roar.

"Well," Mark said, climbing out, "what'd you think?"

Teddy's grin stretched ear to ear. "I think... I think I want to do it again."

Mark laughed, offering a hand to help him down. "Good answer."

They shook hands. It wasn't just a handshake—it felt like an agreement. A beginning.

"You come tomorrow," Mark said. "Same time. We'll make an aerial hunter out of you yet."

"Yes, sir," Teddy said firmly.

As they walked back toward the farmhouse, Teddy looked up at the sky again—so wide, so bright, so full of promises he hadn't known existed yesterday.

He had gone up a boy.

He came down someone else.

Someone who now carried the sky in his blood.

The Naval Reserve Officers Training Corps (NROTC) program was formally established in 1926 as part of the United States' effort to create a broader pipeline of well-educated, commissioned officers. At its outset, the program was placed in six universities across the country, with the intent of giving young men the opportunity to pursue civilian academic degrees while simultaneously preparing for naval service. By the 1930s, as global tensions began to rise, the Navy recognized that the program was not just a supplement but an essential means of cultivating skilled officers. During the 1930s, the NROTC grew in stature and importance as the nation cautiously navigated the challenges of the Depression and the storm clouds of conflict gathering overseas. Naval leadership saw that the future would require officers capable of mastering modern technologies—aviation, radio, gunnery systems, and engineering innovations. For many young men of the era, the program was both a gateway to higher education and a path of service in uncertain times. By combining the rigor of university study with the traditions and expectations of the Navy, the NROTC program created a generation of leaders who would soon be tested in the crucible of World War II.

RESPONSIBILITIES

Teddy woke before dawn, long before the rooster began his rusty crow. He moved carefully around the house, trying not to wake his mother as he dressed, tied the white silk scarf around his neck, and slung the rifle across his shoulder. His father slept in the next room beneath a quilt his mother had sewn the year Teddy was born, his injured leg propped on pillows. Teddy paused a moment at the doorway, watching the rise and fall of his father's chest. The man had worked hard all his life — too hard — and the injury that kept him chairbound still ate at him more deeply than he'd ever admit out loud.

Teddy left quietly.

By the time he reached the field, the horizon was a deep blue smudge that promised sunrise. Mark Sheraton arrived not long after, the familiar hum of the biplane cutting through the morning stillness. This time, Teddy didn't feel the shock of awe or the burst of adrenaline he'd felt on the first day. Instead, there was a calm readiness — a sense that he knew his part now, that he'd earned a place in the second seat.

Mark shut down the engine long enough to lean out and call, "Mornin', sharpshooter. Ready to collect some county money today?"

"Yes, sir," Teddy replied, grinning.

No dramatics, no suspense. The plane rolled. The wheels lifted. They were airborne.

Teddy didn't pay attention to the view this time; he kept his mind steady and focused on the job. They made a wide circuit over the property lines, then dipped low along a stretch of brush at the far edge of Davidson land.

The first coyote appeared near a cluster of rocks. Teddy raised the rifle, braced it, waited for Mark's steadying nod, and fired.

A clean hit. Quick and efficient.

"That's one!" Mark shouted. "County's gonna love you for this!"

They spotted the next two only minutes apart. One trotted near the creek bed; the other lingered by an open pasture. Teddy brought both down with steady hands and precise timing.

Three coyotes in less than fifteen minutes.

As Mark banked the biplane toward home, he called, "That's six dollars the county owes us. Your share's a buck fifty. Nice morning's work."

But the money didn't matter. Teddy barely heard it. He felt something deeper — not pride exactly, but confirmation. He could do this. He could be good at something that wasn't farm chores or school assignments.

They landed. Dust curled. The engine sighed. Teddy climbed down, steady on his feet.

"Same time tomorrow?" Mark asked.

Teddy nodded. "I'll be ready."

When Teddy walked back toward the house, his mother stepped onto the porch, wiping her hands on her apron.

"All three?" she asked.

Teddy nodded. "Yes, ma'am."

She smiled faintly. "Breakfast is ready."

Inside, his father sat at the kitchen table. The morning light caught the tension in his jaw — the same strain that showed whenever he wished he could stand beside his son and couldn't.

"You did good," he said simply.

Teddy sat. His mother served eggs and potatoes, but her eyes kept drifting toward the windows, toward the direction from which the biplane had returned.

"You're gettin' good at that shootin'," his father said.

"Good enough that Sheraton's not wastin' fuel takin' you up there."

Teddy shrugged. "It's mostly Mark. He lines up the shots."

His father shook his head. "No, son. You're the one pullin' the trigger."

After breakfast, Teddy headed to the barn to begin morning chores. The cows were waiting, soft-eyed and patient. Teddy settled into the familiar rhythm of milking, but his thoughts drifted — to the aircraft, to the sky, to the way Mark seemed to take him seriously in a way most grown men rarely did.

College crossed his mind again. His teachers had encouraged it. His mother had hinted at it hopefully. His father had mentioned it quietly while sharpening tools last fall. Teddy wasn't sure what he wanted. College felt far away — like a world he'd read about but never stepped into.

When the milking was done, Teddy carried the buckets toward the barn. His father met him halfway, leaning on his cane.

"You're thinkin' a lot today," his father observed.

Teddy nodded. "Yes, sir."

"Thinkin' about flyin'?"

"Yes, sir."

"And college?"

A pause. "Yes."

His father took a long breath and nodded. "You don't have to choose today. But you do have to think about what you want to become. The world's changin'. Opportunities come and go."

Teddy set the buckets down. "I don't want to leave you and Ma with more work."

His father's voice softened. "We'll manage. We always do. You're not chained here. Don't stay just because you think we need you."

Teddy swallowed. "I don't know what I want yet."

"That's all right," his father said. "Most men don't at your age. But whatever you choose ought to scare you a little. If it doesn't, it's not worth doin'."

They finished chores together — fixing a sagging fence, tending to the animals — and the work grounded them both in familiar routine.

At lunch, Teddy's mother noticed him staring toward the window.

"Are you lookin' for Mr. Sheraton?" she asked kindly.

Teddy smiled shyly. "Just thinkin'."

She set a gentle hand on his shoulder. "Your pa's right. Whatever future you want — college or flyin' — it ought to be your choice. Not ours. And not out of fear."

Her words struck him deeply.

Later that afternoon, Mark rode up on horseback. Three coyote hides were tied to his saddle, proof of the morning's work.

"Well done," Mark said. "County office was impressed. Said it's been a long while since anyone turned in three from one mornin'. You made an impression."

Teddy felt a spark of pride. "So when do I get my share?"

Mark placed the coins in Teddy's hand — a dollar and fifty cents. It felt heavier than the amount deserved, symbolic in a way Teddy couldn't quite articulate.

"Tomorrow?" Mark asked.

Teddy nodded. "Tomorrow."

Mark tipped his hat. "I knew you'd say that."

As Teddy watched Mark ride away into the late-afternoon sun, a realization settled into his bones — quiet, certain, immovable.

Something had begun. Something real.

The chores, the responsibilities, the days spent tending fields and mending fences — they were still pieces of him. Pieces he respected. Pieces that had shaped him.

But the sky had opened a new path. A new feeling. A new future.

And whatever came next, Teddy Davidson knew he would not be the same boy he had been just days before.

In 1938 and 1939, the world stood on the edge of cataclysm. In Europe, Adolf Hitler's Germany had annexed Austria through the Anschluss in March 1938, and just months later, the Munich Agreement permitted Nazi Germany to absorb the Sudetenland from Czechoslovakia. British Prime Minister Neville Chamberlain declared 'peace for our time,' but many doubted the durability of that peace. In March 1939, Hitler violated the agreement by occupying the rest of Czechoslovakia. By September, Germany invaded Poland, prompting Britain and France to declare war. World War II had begun.

Meanwhile in the Pacific, tensions escalated rapidly. Japan had already invaded Manchuria in 1931 and was now deep into its war with China, following the Marco Polo Bridge Incident in 1937. Reports of atrocities, such as the Nanjing Massacre, shocked the global conscience. The United States remained officially neutral, but public concern was growing. Naval build-up and military preparedness increased quietly as policymakers began to consider what a global conflict might mean for American security and values.

THE PATH FORWARD

Teddy tightened the last section of wire on the southern fence line and leaned against the post to test it. It held firm. He exhaled, wiped the sweat from his forehead with the back of his arm, and glanced toward the farmhouse. His father would normally have helped with the fencing, but after the accident, the simplest tasks had become battles for him. Every acre of work, every repair, every daily responsibility had fallen squarely onto Teddy's shoulders.

He didn't complain—complaining didn't mend fences or tend cattle. But sometimes he wondered how much longer he could carry the load of a man's work on a boy's back.

"Teddy!" his mother called from the porch. "Come up here a minute!"

She didn't interrupt unless it was important. Teddy dropped the hammer into the toolbox and walked toward the house, boots kicking up dust. When he climbed the porch steps, his mother handed him his best shirt—clean, pressed, and carefully folded.

"Your father wants you to go see the school principal this afternoon," she said. "Principal Waverly asked to speak with you."

"With me?" Teddy asked, startled. "What for?"

"I don't know," she said, "but he asked for you by name."

That alone meant something.

Teddy washed at the pump, changed shirts, combed his hair, and started the familiar three-mile walk into town. The road stretched straight and quiet, bordered by wheat whispering under the steady Kansas wind. He tried to think of a reason the principal might want to see him, but nothing came to mind.

The schoolhouse stood on a slight rise at the edge of town, its white paint bright under the sun. As Teddy approached, Principal Waverly stepped out the front door, waiting as though expecting him.

"Afternoon, Teddy," he said, smiling warmly. "Come on inside."

Teddy removed his cap and followed him into the office. Principal Waverly sat behind his desk but leaned forward, resting both forearms on the wood. His expression was thoughtful, serious.

"You're probably wonderin' why I called you here."

"Yes, sir," Teddy said.

Principal Waverly studied him for a moment. "Teddy... you've taken on more responsibility this past year than most grown men. I know about your father's injury. I know you've been runnin' that farm alone."

Teddy lowered his eyes.

"I also know you quit baseball," Waverly continued. "Not because you wanted to, but because the family needed you."

That stung more than Teddy liked to admit. Baseball had been the one thing that made him feel alive. But quitting hadn't felt like a decision—it had felt like inevitability.

"And I know," Principal Waverly said gently, "that you dropped out of school for a time. Most boys don't come back from that. But you did."

Teddy swallowed.

"And even with all your responsibilities, you've kept your schooling going. You finished your homework on time. You walked your assignments to school yourself, even after twelve-hour days. You turned in every exam in person. You studied late at night under a lantern when most boys your age were asleep. And your grades never slipped."

Teddy looked up, surprised. "I didn't realize anyone noticed."

"I notice," Principal Waverly said. "And so will others."

He opened a drawer and pulled out a pamphlet—a navy-blue cover embossed with a gold crest.

Naval Reserve Officers' Training Corps

Georgia Institute of Technology

Teddy stared at it.

"I believe you're suited for more than farm life," Waverly said quietly. "You have a mind for engineering. You have discipline, and you understand sacrifice. And now that your father is gettin' steadier on his feet, this is the moment to think about your future."

Teddy's heart thudded. "I always figured college was for boys who had the means."

"College is for boys who have the ability," Waverly corrected. "And you have plenty of that."

He pushed the pamphlet across the desk.

"The Navy is looking for young men who already know responsibility. Georgia Tech is looking for young men who can handle challenge. I believe you fit both."

Teddy swallowed hard. "What would I have to do?"

"We'll begin the application tomorrow," Waverly replied. "You'll need records, recommendations, a physical, and then... an interview."

"An interview?" Teddy echoed.

"Yes," Waverly said with a smile. "And you'll do just fine."

The following week felt like a windstorm of paperwork, signatures, and questions. Teddy filled out forms at the kitchen table, signing his name with careful strokes. His mother pressed his shirts and ironed a collar that hadn't seen daylight in years. His father, though still weak, sat with him every evening.

"You tell 'em exactly who you are," his father said. "Don't hide the hard parts. Hard parts are what make a man."

Teddy nodded.

He continued tending the farm while preparing for the interview. He dropped off homework and exams at the school whenever he passed through town. In the evenings, he studied algebra and mechanical principles under lamplight, sometimes fighting sleep, sometimes winning.

When the interview day arrived, Teddy boarded the bus to Wichita wearing his best shirt and his father's old tie. The road was long and dusty. He held a folder containing his transcripts, recommendation letters, and the carefully prepared application.

The Naval officer who greeted him was tall, stern, and direct. The questions were difficult, probing.

"Explain a time you took responsibility."

"How do you handle hardship?"

"What do you know of discipline?"

"What sacrifices have you made?"

Teddy answered honestly.

He talked about the farm.

About long hours and long nights.

About quitting baseball.

About dropping out and returning.

About running a household while keeping up with school.

About walking homework into town after exhausting days.

About wanting to do something meaningful.

The officer listened quietly, then gave a single nod.

"You have determination, son. The Navy respects that."

On the bus ride home, Teddy wondered whether determination alone could carry him where he hoped to go.

Three weeks later, he returned from the fields to find his mother on the porch, an envelope pressed to her chest. Her eyes shone.

"Teddy... it's here."

His father stood beside her, leaning on his cane.

Teddy opened the letter carefully.

We are pleased to inform you that you have been accepted into the Naval Reserve Officers' Training Corps at the Georgia Institute of Technology...

He reread the line three times before it sank in.

His mother burst into tears. His father's face broke into a smile that made him look ten years younger.

"You did it, son," he said proudly. "By God, you did it."

"I... I can't believe it," Teddy whispered.

"Believe it," his father replied. "You earned every bit of this."

The summer that followed was full of preparation. Teddy wanted the farm in solid condition before he left, so he worked harder than ever—reinforcing fences, repairing equipment, stacking feed, organizing tools, making sure everything would run as smoothly as possible.

His father grew stronger each week. He still needed a cane, but he could help now—feeding livestock, sorting tools, walking the perimeter.

"You're not stayin' here," his father told him one afternoon. "The farm'll be fine. And so will we. Don't let worry keep you from your future."

Teddy nodded, though the knot in his chest stayed.

His mother packed his suitcase slowly, methodically. She folded shirts with care, checked buttons, stitched up a loose seam, tucked extra socks in the corners. Once, Teddy caught her holding one of his shirts to her cheek, eyes closed.

"Promise me you'll write," she whispered.

"I will, Ma."

"You'll be far away," she said, brushing his hair back. "But you'll still be ours."

On a warm August morning, Teddy stood at the station with his small suitcase. The wheat shimmered gold in the early light. His father stood beside him, leaning less on his cane than ever.

"You carried this family when we needed you most," he said, placing a firm hand on Teddy's shoulder. "Now go carry yourself."

His mother hugged him tightly. "We love you, Teddy. Go make yourself proud."

When the train approached with a deep rolling thunder, steam billowed around the platform. Teddy climbed aboard, turned, and saw his parents standing side by side—two figures small against the wide Kansas sky.

He pressed his hand to the window as the train pulled away.

The fields rolled past. His home receded behind him.

And for the first time in his life, Teddy Davidson felt the horizon pulling him forward instead of holding him in place.

He was going to Georgia Tech.

He was going into the Navy.

He was stepping into the man he was meant to become.

On September 1st, 1939, Adolf Hitler's Luftwaffe bombed Warsaw, Poland, unleashing a ferocious air assault that shocked the world. Shortly thereafter, German ground forces crossed the border, launching a full-scale invasion under the doctrine of Blitzkrieg—swift, mechanized, and ruthless.

The next day, Great Britain, France, Australia, and New Zealand declared war on Germany, honoring their commitments to Poland and signaling the start of a global conflict. World War II had begun in earnest, plunging the world's great powers into a confrontation that would reshape history.

In the United States, official neutrality remained intact, but public concern deepened. For young men like Teddy Davidson, already in uniform and training for service, the war in Europe no longer felt distant—it was becoming a question of when, not if, America would be drawn in.

GEORGIA TECH SUMMER AT SEA

By the time Teddy Davidson reached his sophomore year at Georgia Tech, he had developed a hard-earned routine. The regimen of Naval ROTC, academic excellence, and physical demands pushed him far beyond the average college student. His days began at dawn with PT—Physical Training—on the parade ground. He ran drills, did calisthenics, and then headed straight to classes in engineering, mathematics, and military science. By mid-afternoon, he was already exhausted, but there was still drill practice, inspections, and meetings with senior midshipmen. On weekends, while others might relax or sleep in, Teddy was often studying or helping lead underclassman field exercises.

Teddy's course load was not for the faint of heart. He took courses in thermodynamics, calculus, navigation, and aeronautical mechanics. There were days when he would wake up with textbooks in his lap and a dull ache in his temples from falling asleep mid-equation. Professors were demanding, and ROTC instructors even more so. His uniform had to be spotless, his rifle gleaming, and his posture perfect.

But Teddy found satisfaction in the rigor. He welcomed the structure, and he pushed himself to be the best in every category. He wasn't the tallest or the loudest midshipman, but he stood out for his quiet competence and growing confidence. It helped that he had natural leadership instincts—other students often turned to him for clarification on difficult assignments or for guidance during drills.

That summer, he was assigned to the USS Langley, an aging carrier serving as a training platform for future aviators and officers. As part of the Langley's rotation, Teddy had to spend time in each major department: navigation, engineering, aircraft handling, and even damage control and fire suppression. He spent several days below deck with the engine room crew, learning about the internal systems of the ship. Later, he rotated to the flight deck, where he observed aircraft landings and takeoffs, learned basic tower communications, and participated in aircraft spotting drills. The carrier was bustling with activity, and Teddy absorbed every bit of it like a sponge.

One day, during a simulated emergency, Teddy and three other midshipmen had to seal off a lower compartment and handle a mock fire. They worked quickly, following Navy protocol, and managed to impress the Chief Petty Officer overseeing the drill. That same week, he helped direct dummy munitions movement below deck, coordinating between ordnance officers and the tower.

Although the Langley had once seen real action, by this point she served as a floating classroom. Still, the weight of history clung to her like salt air. Teddy would stand alone on the fantail at night, staring at the wake trailing behind them, dreaming of what was to come.

The following summer brought an entirely different experience: Naval Air Station Pensacola.

There, Teddy wasn't flying yet—but he was getting close. As part of the pipeline toward becoming a naval aviator, he spent his summer rotation shadowing hangar operations, learning logistics of aircraft parts, repair schedules, and pilot readiness procedures. It was as much about organization as it was about aircraft. He worked with enlisted crewmen responsible for keeping the trainers airworthy and ready for the next generation of fliers.

He also received additional instruction in tower operations, meteorology, aircraft fueling and loading protocols, and participated in mock readiness exercises. One assignment had him coordinating between logistics and flight scheduling to ensure that the correct aircraft were available for a mock carrier prep drill. Everything had to run like clockwork—or the officer in charge would deliver a chewing-out that no one soon forgot.

By the end of his junior year, Teddy had earned the admiration of his instructors. He had shown a deep understanding of naval operations beyond just flying—he understood the system that made aviation work. And he knew how critical every cog in the machine was, from the guy on the flight deck holding the batons to the mechanics below deck hunting down a faulty hydraulic line.

It was clear: Teddy Davidson was more than just a student. He was becoming a leader. And soon, the cockpit would call.

One of the great advantages America carried into the inevitable Second World War was the character of its youth. Raised in a nation of vast distances, mechanical innovation, and individual responsibility, young Americans had developed a strong sense of independence, problem-solving, and self-reliance. Many had grown up driving and repairing cars, managing farm equipment, and making do with what they had.

This culture of hands-on ingenuity translated directly into the battlefield. American soldiers, sailors, and airmen not only followed orders—they adapted. When machinery broke, they fixed it. When leadership fell, they stepped up. When the path forward was unclear, they found one. It was not blind obedience that made America strong in war —it was a disciplined kind of freedom. The kind that says, if one falls, another rises. And it gave America an edge no enemy could replicate.

THE DANCE OF THE MARKSMAN

It was the fall of his senior year, and Teddy Davidson finally gave in to the suggestion of his roommates and fellow midshipmen to attend the campus mixer. He hadn't had a social life to speak of since becoming a midshipman. His time had been consumed by drills, lectures, watches, and weekends filled with naval obligations. But that evening, as twilight cast long shadows across the red-brick walkways of Georgia Tech, he put on his uniform, straightened his cover, and made his way to the ballroom.

The room was alive with sound. A jazz band played

upbeat swing, their brass instruments gleaming under the soft chandeliers. Cadets and civilians alike crowded the floor. Laughter, movement, perfume, and aftershave mingled in the air. Teddy removed his cover and placed it on a long table near the entrance, already crowded with dozens of others. He stood a moment, taking it all in.

He moved through the crowd with purpose but no particular destination. When the music paused and people shifted, Teddy turned to head toward the door—when he collided with someone.

She was stunning. Long brunette hair, sharp cheekbones, and piercing blue eyes. "Sailor, aren't you going to apologize?" she asked.

"Yes, ma'am," Teddy replied. "I just didn't see you."

"I see. So, you're not only rude, but also blind."

"Would you like to dance?" he asked with a hopeful smile.

She gave a small nod. "I've got room on my dance card for one."

Teddy wasn't much of a dancer. She led. He followed—awkward at first, then with more confidence as he relaxed into her rhythm. She laughed quietly once when he stepped slightly wrong, but she never scolded. Her eyes sparkled with patient amusement.

When the song ended, he looked at her and said, "Would you like to get some air?"

She nodded. "I was hoping you'd ask."

They stepped out onto a stone balcony overlooking the lawn. The night was clear and cool. The stars had emerged above the Atlanta skyline. They walked slowly beneath the portico, their footsteps soft.

"So," she said, "how does a Kansas farm boy end up at Georgia Tech in a Navy uniform?"

Teddy smiled. "You did some research."

"Not much. You just give off that practical, self-reliant air. And your vowels are pure Midwest."

Teddy chuckled. "Guilty on all counts. I was supposed to be a ballplayer. All-State. Then my dad got hurt. Had to take over the farm. Missed most of senior year. Still managed to graduate. Principal helped me find a way out—Naval ROTC. Tuition, room, and board. Plus, I've always wanted to fly."

"You're in the aviation track?"

"Applied to Pensacola for flight school. Hoping to hear back. We'll see."

She looked impressed. "That's serious business."

"I figure if you're going to serve, serve with wings."

"I like that."

"What about you?" Teddy asked. "You look... like you have options."

She laughed. "That's very diplomatic. I'm Caroline McKenna. My father owns McKenna Textiles, so yes, I've had some options. I'm a junior, studying education. I want to teach."

"Kids?"

"High school. History. Literature."

"That explains the vocabulary."

She gave him a sideways glance. "What about yours?"

"Books were our escape back home. Steinbeck, Hemingway, Churchill. I read when the animals were fed and the chores were done."

"I like that," she said. "You're not what I expected."

"What were you expecting?"

She shrugged. "Something cockier. The uniform, the square jaw. But you're... observant."

He smiled. "That's one way to say cautious."

"No," she said. "You listen. Most boys don't."

They kept walking.

He said, "You ever thought of flying?"

She paused. "What makes you ask that?"

"I don't know. You just seem unafraid."

She tilted her head. "I don't think you're wrong. But that's a story for another night."

He didn't push.

He told her the story of gunnery school—how he had been issued a standard-issue Springfield rifle, like every other midshipman. Most of these rifles had seen countless training cycles, handled by generations of cadets. The rifling—the spiral grooves cut into the barrel designed to impart spin on the bullet—was severely worn on many of them. And when the rifling wears out, a bullet doesn't rotate properly. Without that gyroscopic spin, it wobbles in flight, drifts, and can veer slightly off course.

Most cadets were allowed five practice shots to understand how their particular rifle was behaving. Only after those calibration rounds would the instructors begin scoring. But Teddy, frugal by nature and dead-serious about marksmanship, declined the full set of five. 'One will do,' he'd told the instructor. The instructor chuckled. 'You'll need more than that, son.' But Teddy lay prone, focused, and squeezed off a single shot. He felt it immediately. The lack of clean spin. He adjusted instinctively—recalibrating where the shot landed, factoring in the barrel's wear.

When they began the scored sequence, Teddy fired his rounds with unwavering calm. One after another, tight groupings formed on the target. Instructors gathered behind him, whispering in disbelief. No one shot expert on their first attempt—especially not with those old rifles. But Teddy did. Because he could sense where the bullet would go—not where it should go, but where it would go. That made all the difference.

Caroline listened, captivated. 'So, you just knew?' she asked.

'You grow up hunting coyotes with a bolt-action .22,' he said, 'you learn to make every shot count. A bad shot is a wasted opportunity—and sometimes, a lost calf.'

"You're frugal," she said. "And disciplined."

"Bullets cost money."

She smiled. "You're not like anyone I've ever met."

They talked about professors and courses, books and weather, the smell of cotton bales, the loneliness of dorms, the oddness of cafeteria food. They lingered near the lanterns along the walkway, voices softer now, as if the night could hear.

When they finally reached her dorm steps, he stepped aside and looked up at the building.

"Thank you for tonight," she said.

"Thank you for the conversation," he said.

"I hope we'll do this again."

"If you'll let me."

She paused. "I think I will."

He gave a nod. "Good night, Miss McKenna."

"Good night, Mr. Davidson."

And she disappeared behind the door.

Teddy turned back toward the quad, hands in his coat pockets, heart steady, mind racing.

The inevitability of war seemed farther away.

In 1939, Hitler's claims of limited ambition were exposed as lies. Meanwhile, Italy continued its imperial expansion, aligning more closely with Nazi Germany. In Britain, Prime Minister Chamberlain's policy of appeasement collapsed under growing public doubt, with voices like Winston Churchill rising in urgency.

Japan, already entrenched in war with China, pressed deeper into the Pacific, seeking resources and strategic control. Isolated by great oceans on both sides, the United States was reluctant to get involved. While President Roosevelt closely followed global events, most Americans resisted involvement, still haunted by the losses of World War I. Yet the world was shifting, and war would not remain distant forever.

UNPLANNED LOVE

Teddy Davidson had always lived his life by design.

From his earliest memories, every move had been purposeful. He learned early that nothing good came without effort, and he never expected luck to pave his way. He earned what he had. The plan had always been simple: excel in school, dominate on the baseball field, earn a scholarship, and become an engineer. His father's injury had threatened to derail that plan, but Teddy adjusted, adapted. That's what he did. He became a Naval ROTC midshipman. Now his dream was to fly—apply his love of engineering to the sky.

His days were governed by orders, inspections, early reveille, and evening taps. It was rigorous and exact, and that suited him just fine. He didn't need freedom; he needed direction.

Until Caroline.

She, too, had constructed her life with discipline and vision. A daughter of privilege, she could have followed leisure, but she'd chosen education. Literature and history called to her, and she saw herself standing at the front of a classroom, inspiring minds the way a few teachers had once inspired her. Though undeniably beautiful—head-turning, even—she had little interest in boys. Most of them were immature, transparently self-centered, and utterly incapable of grasping who she was. She didn't play games, and she wasn't going to waste her time pretending otherwise.

Then Teddy quite literally ran into her.

Their connection had unfolded like pages in a well-loved novel—each chapter a bit more daring than the last. At first, it was glances across the dining hall, then shared laughs over a Coke. Soon, their paths seemed to bend toward each other. Their daily schedules offered slivers of time, but in those moments, they found meaning. A hand touched a forearm longer than necessary. Fingers brushed while reaching for the same napkin. Her leg nudged his under a shared table and didn't move.

There were no declarations. Just tension. Subtle. Electric. Inescapable.

On a bright Sunday morning, Caroline appeared in her father's cream-colored Lincoln convertible. Her hair was down, waving in the breeze like silk caught in the wind. Her eyes sparkled as she walked toward him outside the chapel.

"Jump in, sailor," she said with a grin.

He did, grinning back. "Where to?"

"You'll see. I packed a picnic."

They drove away from the university town, the sunlight falling warm on their arms, the wind lifting Caroline's hair in wild curls. She drove confidently, one hand on the wheel, the other occasionally resting near his on the seat.

The silence between them wasn't awkward. It was full—of thoughts, of anticipation, of curiosity neither quite knew how to name.

After a winding half hour, Caroline turned onto a shaded dirt path that climbed to a quiet hilltop. The view was breathtaking—rolling hills fading into a green valley below. There wasn't another soul in sight.

Caroline laid out the blanket with practiced grace and unpacked fried chicken, biscuits, and glass bottles of Coke. She looked radiant, framed by sunlight and surrounded by open sky.

"Are you hungry, sailor?" she teased.

"Always," Teddy replied, laughing. "This looks better than anything I've seen in the mess hall."

They ate, talked, laughed. He told her about inspection day disasters and how upperclassmen liked to call plebes "seaweeds." She told him about her students back home, the novels she hoped to teach someday. Then they lay side by side in silence, watching clouds roll slowly overhead.

She reached out and brushed a breadcrumb from his cheek, her hand lingering. He caught her wrist gently and pulled her close.

Their kiss was not a surprise. It was a culmination.

It began slowly—tender, exploratory. But as they gave themselves over to it, everything else fell away. Time collapsed into a singular moment of touch, breath, and need.

Teddy's hands moved to her waist, feeling her warmth through the fabric. Caroline pulled him closer, her fingers threading through the hair at the base of his neck. Her blouse came away with each button, her skin golden and soft beneath. He leaned in and kissed her collarbone, then the hollow of her throat.

She responded without hesitation. Her hands slid beneath his shirt, exploring his chest, tracing the lines of muscle and the trail of hair downward. When he pressed against her, she welcomed him, guiding his body closer.

Her breast fit into his hand like it had always belonged there. She gasped softly as he caressed her, thumb grazing her nipple, her back arching slightly in reply. She guided him with her body, pulling him into rhythm.

One by one, clothes came away, discarded into the grass like dried petals. They paused only once, eyes locked.

"You're sure?" he asked.

"I've never been more," she whispered, pulling him toward her.

He entered her with reverence. She inhaled sharply— more from emotion than discomfort—and wrapped her legs around him. They moved gently at first, then more urgently. He kissed her shoulder, her cheek, her lips, and she met every motion with breathless abandon. Her hands clutched his back, nails grazing his skin, pulling him deeper.

Their bodies folded together, one motion, one rhythm, one rising current. When release came, it was not just physical—it was emotional, spiritual. A surrender. A revelation.

After, they lay tangled in each other's arms, hearts pounding in sync.

"I didn't plan this," she whispered.

"Neither did I," he said, brushing her hair from her face.

They dressed slowly, helping each other with gentle touches and small laughs. Caroline packed up the picnic. Teddy folded the blanket.

Neither spoke much as they descended the hill. The car ride back was full of stolen glances, half-smiles, and long stretches of silence that said more than words ever could.

Teddy watched the curve of Caroline's face as she drove. He saw the same bewilderment he felt reflected in her expression. What had happened wasn't just a step forward—it was a leap. A fall. And he wasn't sure if they'd landed or were still tumbling.

He rested his hand on hers. She didn't pull away.

Caroline glanced at him. "Do you think this changes everything?"

"I think it already did," he said.

She nodded. "I wasn't looking for this."

"I wasn't either."

"But I'm not sorry," she whispered.

"Me neither."

When they reached campus, Caroline parked behind one of the academic halls. They sat for a moment, neither making a move.

"I should... go study," she said.

"I should go clean my rifle," he said.

They both laughed.

Then Teddy leaned in—not for a kiss, just to rest his forehead against hers. "Whatever this is, we're in it together. Okay?"

She nodded, eyes closed. "Okay."

He stepped out, closed the door, and walked away, knowing something inside him had changed.

And in the distance, a world drifted ever closer to war.

But for now, for this moment, love—unplanned and unasked for—was real.

SPRING FORMAL

By spring of 1940, Hitler and his staff had finalized plans for the invasion of Western Europe. In April, they put those plans into motion with the swift invasions of Denmark and Norway, securing key ports and resource routes. Meanwhile, Great Britain was preparing. for war, increasing mobilization and strengthening its defenses. In the Pacific, Japanese aggression continued, with British territories undermanned and vulnerable. In the United States, talk of war remained quiet. The memory of World War I still lingered, and most Americans were reluctant to support involvement. Few were willing to speak out, as isolationism held firm.

SO MANY QUESTIONS

Senior year was sprinting by like a fastball out of the hand. Teddy Davidson barely had time to blink between classes, drills, inspections, and papers, and suddenly it was December. By now, he had a reputation on campus—sharp-minded, steady, a leader in both the classroom and on the drill field. His professors praised his essays. His gunnery instructors joked about him being a "sure shot with a sure future." The Naval ROTC program posted monthly rankings, and Teddy's name was consistently near the top.

Though the curriculum remained grueling—naval engineering, leadership theory, and endless hours of physical training—Teddy handled it with growing confidence. He was no longer just the farm kid from Kansas. He was Midshipman Davidson now. His classmates turned to him for guidance, and the officers took note. His future seemed all but written in blue and gold. But even with all the accolades, Teddy still found himself thinking about Caroline.

They met when time allowed, often slipping away on weekends for long walks or study sessions that turned into laughter and kisses. With her, the pressure faded. Her voice, her confidence, and her mischievous smile gave him something to look forward to beyond drills and grades. He hadn't told her yet, but he knew. He loved her.

That Christmas, Teddy returned to Kansas. The snow was light that year, just a soft powder across the fields. At home, his mother fussed over his uniform while his father asked careful questions about gunnery ranges and Navy life.

One evening, after dinner, Teddy sat alone with his mother by the fire. The house was quiet except for the ticking of the clock.

"She sounds lovely, this Caroline," his mother said, darning one of his father's socks with steady hands. "You talk about her like... like your eyes are always looking east."

Teddy smiled, then looked down at the floor. "She is lovely. Smart. Brave."

His mother looked up. "Do you love her?"

He hesitated only a second. "Yes," he said softly. "I do."

She set the sock down. "Have you told her?"

"No," he said. "Not yet. But I probably should.

His mother just nodded, her eyes shining a little, and went back to her needle.

Down in Georgia, Caroline had her own fireside conversation. Her mother, ever the genteel Southern hostess, had cornered her daughter in the parlor with a pot of tea and a knowing smile.

"You've been humming," her mother said, passing a cup. "You only hum when there's a man."

Caroline laughed. "I suppose I have."

"Does he love you?"

"I believe he does."

"Has he told you?"

Caroline shook her head. "Not yet. But I don't need him to say it just to know."

Her father entered the room with a book tucked under his arm. "I like the sound of this boy," he said. "Tell me he's not a Yale man."

"Worse," Caroline teased. "Georgia Tech."

Her parents chuckled, but beneath it all, they saw the truth. Their daughter was serious. And they didn't press her further.

Returning in January, the cold Atlantic wind swept across the Georgia Tech campus, but Teddy felt warmer somehow. Caroline was waiting at the station when he arrived, her scarf fluttering in the wind, her eyes bright beneath her cap. They embraced quickly, then lingered in a silence so full it could burst.

That winter was a season of closeness. They stole moments amid exams and marches. Their lovemaking deepened, not just in frequency, but in meaning. They

had come to know each other's rhythms, likes, and long-
ings. They learned not only how to love, but how to give
pleasure and how to receive it. Teddy knew the places
along Caroline's collarbone where her breath caught.
Caroline understood how to run her fingers through his
hair in a way that made him sigh into her neck.

They explored each other with a growing trust,
becoming fluent in a language spoken in sighs and skin.
There was laughter sometimes, and other times quiet
stillness—limbs entwined, hearts thudding in sync.
When they parted at night, it was always with a glance
that said: Soon.

Spring arrived, and with it, the much-anticipated
Midshipmen's Spring Formal in Atlanta. The Peachtree
Ballroom was resplendent with bunting and Navy flags,
and a big band played swing numbers while cadets and
their dates circled the polished floor. Caroline wore a silk
gown the color of moonlight. Teddy had never seen her
look more luminous.

After dinner, they danced slowly to a softer tune.
The lights had dimmed slightly, and the smell of roses
hung in the air. Teddy held her close, her head just below
his chin, and finally let the words slip free.

"I love you," he said.

She didn't respond right away. Her cheek pressed
into his shoulder.

"I don't know what the future holds," he continued.
"The Navy, war maybe, a thousand miles of ocean. So
many questions I don't have answers to. But I want you
in my life."

She looked up at him, eyes full of light. "I love you

too," she whispered. "We'll figure it out, Teddy. Whatever the world throws at us—we'll face it together."

They kissed, and the music rose around them, strings and horns swirling like stars.

Later, in a quiet hotel room above the city, they undressed in silence, not from nerves but reverence. Teddy unfastened each clasp of her gown as if he were unwrapping something sacred. Caroline reached for his collar, her fingers working each button slowly, her eyes never leaving his. They stood together in the hush, bare and unashamed, before slipping beneath the sheets.

Their mouths met first—long, lingering kisses that deepened with every breath. Teddy's hands moved over her like memory and desire entwined, learning her all over again. Caroline responded with soft gasps and fingers that roamed with confidence, finding the places he didn't know he had missed.

They moved together with practiced intimacy—familiar yet never routine. Teddy pressed his lips to the soft curve of her shoulder; Caroline arched to meet him. Her hand guided him, their eyes locking as their bodies joined. They took their time, shifting, exploring, holding, until the rhythm between them became instinctive.

Caroline whispered his name in a tone that trembled between joy and need. Teddy answered with kisses, with hands that held her tightly, then gently. They reached for each other again and again, touching not just skin, but soul.

When it was done, they remained wrapped together, his hand resting over her heart, her head nestled beneath his chin. The warmth between them was not just physical. It was earned.

"I love you," she whispered.

"I love you," he said, brushing her hair from her cheek.

They said it again. And again. Until words gave way to breathing, and breathing gave way to sleep.

ENABLE AIR STATION

In May of 1940, Hitler introduced to the world the concept of Blitzkrieg—lightning war. Speed, surprise, and coordination were its hallmarks, and it stunned even the most seasoned generals. Aviators in the U.S. military watched with great interest as Germany deployed ground-attack aircraft like the Junkers JU-87, better known as the Stuka dive bomber. These planes coordinated closely with fast-moving armored divisions, essentially becoming artillery from the air. The Germans were rapidly learning how to wage a new kind of mechanized war. The French and British were about to learn devastating lessons on the receiving end. And across the Atlantic, American commanders, pilots, and trainees tried to learn vicariously—hoping they would have time to prepare for what seemed increasingly inevitable.

WINGS TO THE FUTURE

Theodore R. Davidson stood tall, his heart thudding in his chest as he stepped forward across the stage. The hall echoed with polite applause and the proud voice of the announcer rang out: "Theodore R. Davidson, with distinction. Class Rank: Number Three."

He grasped the diploma with a firm hand, his dress whites crisp and brilliant under the auditorium lights. Somewhere in the crowd, Caroline clapped with genuine pride, seated between her parents and his own. It was 1940, and Georgia Tech's Naval ROTC program was producing a new batch of ensigns for a world that teetered on the brink of war.

Mr. Davidson, stiff-backed in a borrowed suit, kept

his hands clasped together tightly in his lap. He didn't trust them not to shake. Seeing his boy cross that stage—a boy who had once fallen asleep under a tractor with grease on his face—left him humbled and speechless. He wasn't a man of flowery words. But he'd never felt prouder. "He did this," he thought. "He earned every bit of it. And he did it clean." The war ahead terrified him. But today, he allowed pride to override fear.

Mrs. Davidson dabbed at the corner of her eye with a handkerchief. She remembered the night Teddy told them he wanted to fly. She'd been afraid then. Still was. But now, watching him—strong, sharp, resolute—she no longer saw just her son. She saw a man America would one day be grateful for his service.

Beside them, Caroline's mother adjusted her silk gloves, her mind quietly appraising the family seated next to her. Rough hands, simple speech—but full of dignity. And their son? He was clearly exceptional. As for Caroline, she hadn't stopped smiling since the ceremony began. The way she looked at him—there was more than admiration there. There was commitment. Real and deep.

Mr. McKenna leaned forward slightly, elbow resting on his knee. He wasn't a man easily impressed. But this boy—this Kansas farm boy—had something. Integrity, polish, a sense of gravity. He'd come from nothing and turned it into something solid. And somehow, he'd won his daughter's heart without ever trying to impress him. "That's a man," he thought.

Outside, beneath an arch of magnolias, the two families gathered. Mr. Davidson shook Caroline's father's hand—solid, respectful. Caroline's mother, elegant and warm, complimented Teddy's achievements. It was their first meeting, but one laced with the awareness that their children were building something strong and lasting. Both families sensed it, even if no formal promises had yet been made.

As they chatted in the dappled sunlight, Caroline slipped her hand into Teddy's. No one commented on it. They didn't need to. Everyone saw what it meant.

That evening, as the sun dipped low and the air carried a touch of summer, Caroline and Teddy sat on a bench just beyond the old engineering building. They held hands in the soft hush of twilight.

"We could get engaged," Teddy said quietly. "But I don't want to make you wait through the unknown."

"I don't want a ring to be a burden," Caroline answered. "I want it to be a promise made when the time is right."

They agreed—no engagement, no formal commitment. Just love, and the promise of a future they hoped to build.

The next morning, Caroline accompanied Teddy to the station. The train hissed with steam, ready to bear its passengers south. She hugged him tightly, then whispered into his ear, "I'm not fond of these goodbye kisses, and I know they're going to happen again and again as we lead our life together. It's something I'll have to get used to—and I will. But for now... again, a kiss goodbye."

She leaned in and kissed him, tender and lingering, then stepped back.

Just before the train pulled away, she added, "When you come back, I'll have a surprise for you."

Teddy watched the platform drift past, her figure growing smaller, framed by mist and morning sun. He leaned back in his seat and let the rhythm of the train take him. His mind wandered to flights over Kansas fields, the smell of crop dust in the air, and Caroline's voice in the wind.

Pensacola Naval Air Station awaited.

PENSACOLA FLA

Most of the World War activity was in Europe in the fall of 1940. The evacuation of Dunkirk, the continued aggression by Italian forces, and Churchill's spectacular speeches kept media attention firmly on the European theater. But quietly, across the Pacific, storm clouds were gathering. Britain began withdrawing from Singapore and other imperial territories, while Japan, emboldened and unopposed, continued to expand its reach across the Pacific south of the Japanese mainland. Few in America realized that another war was already taking shape—one that would soon redraw the maps of Asia and bring the United States into a second front.

WINGS IN TRAINING

The sun baked the tarmac at Naval Air Station Pensacola as a line of SNJ Texan trainers shimmered in the morning haze. Teddy Davidson stood among the other cadets in his khakis, helmet tucked under one arm, boots polished, heart racing. The thrill of the sky had never been closer.

Flight instruction had moved beyond ground school and classroom lectures. Now, it was stick time. Every day brought a new maneuver, a new lesson in the controlled violence of naval aviation. And today promised the most exciting session yet—combat maneuvering.

Their instructor, Lieutenant Commander Paulson, had the rough voice of a man raised in cockpits and salted by Pacific air. He paced before them in his faded leather flight jacket, tapping a pointer against a blackboard covered in aerial arcs and loops.

"Today," he barked, "you'll be introduced to basic

aerial combat maneuvers. These aren't for fun. These will keep you alive if a Zero's on your tail."

Teddy leaned forward, absorbing every word.

Paulson outlined the classic Split-S—an inverted half-roll followed by a descending half-loop that reversed direction. Then came the Chandelle, a climbing turn used to gain altitude while reversing course. The Cuban Eight, the Barrel Roll, the Lazy Eight.

And then, the Immelmann.

"This one," Paulson said, circling the chalked diagram like it was a curse, "is a half-loop followed by a half-roll. It converts speed into altitude and reverses your direction. Executed correctly, you'll find yourself flying the opposite direction, higher and faster. But done wrong—and it'll stall your bird."

His eyes roved over the cadets until they landed squarely on Teddy.

"Do not—repeat, do not—attempt an Immelmann on your own. Understood?"

"Yes, sir!" the cadets barked.

Teddy nodded too, though a flicker of curiosity sparked in him. The Immelmann seemed so elegant. So, daring. So...Teddy.

That afternoon, Teddy and his assigned instructor, Ensign Garrity, taxied out to the runway in their SNJ. Garrity handled takeoff, then handed the controls over at 3,000 feet.

"You've got the stick, Davidson. Let's see a clean turn to port."

Teddy eased into the maneuver, feeling the response

of the controls. Each adjustment translated instantly to the aircraft's posture. It was like dancing with the wind.

They ran drills: coordinated turns, shallow dives, a gentle climb. Garrity had Teddy try a basic wingover—a half-loop climbing turn that bled speed while repositioning. Teddy managed it decently, though he came out a touch low.

After landing, Garrity gave him a brief critique. "Keep your pitch gentler coming out of the loop. But good instincts."

"Thank you, sir."

Garrity left him with a nod and headed back toward the hangars. The next scheduled flight was solo—supervised only by tower communication. Teddy's name was up.

The solo hop came two days later. Teddy suited up early and reviewed his checklist twice. He was cleared for basic aerial drills at 5,000 feet and above. The air was cool and calm, perfect flying weather.

Once airborne, the SNJ purred beneath him like a trusted friend. He banked gently, rising into a long arc above the Gulf. The blue horizon stretched forever.

He ran his drills cleanly: a slow climb, a power-on stall recovery, a descending spiral. Confidence surged. He felt one with the plane.

Then, the voice echoed from memory.

*"Do not attempt an Immelmann on your own."

But now... wasn't that exactly the test? To push limits? Wasn't that what pilots did?

Teddy banked right, gained speed in a shallow dive, then pulled hard into a vertical climb. The SNJ rose sharply. He reached the apex—and instinctively began the half-roll.

The sky tilted.

The controls went sluggish.

The nose dropped.

And the engine sputtered.

He had stalled.

Panic punched him in the chest. The aircraft trembled, nose-down, spinning gently.

He reacted: throttle back, rudder neutral, ailerons steady. The SNJ responded—slowly, then with more bite. Airspeed returned.

Altitude was bleeding fast.

He leveled the wings. Pulled gently. The Gulf approached like a drawn curtain.

Then—lift.

She caught.

Teddy stabilized at 2,000 feet. He was breathing hard, sweat dripping under his goggles. His gloves were damp.

He circled, testing all controls. No damage. Systems normal.

He climbed back to 5,000 feet, flying gentle patterns for another fifteen minutes—enough to show flight time had passed.

Then he returned to base, greased the landing, taxied, and parked.

Later, Garrity reviewed the log.

"Looks like you cut it a little short, Davidson."

"Felt a little turbulence," Teddy said, keeping his tone even. "Didn't want to push it."

Garrity nodded slowly. "Smart. Stay inside your envelope. We'll start loops next week."

"Yes, sir."

Teddy walked away, shaken but emboldened. He had flown the edge—and made it back.

But next time, he thought, he'd do it right.

NAVY
NAVY
NAVY
NAVY
NAVY
NAVY
NAVY
NAVY

By late 1940, world headlines remained fixed on the rapid and stunning advances of the Third Reich across Europe. Hitler's armies had swept through the continent with alarming speed, reshaping borders and shattering the illusion of peace. Meanwhile, in Asia, Japan continued its relentless assault on China. In response, the Burma Road was opened to provide overland supply routes to the embattled Chinese forces, as naval access had been largely severed by Japanese control of the seas. Despite these escalating tensions in the Pacific, American public attention remained centered on Europe. The notion of a war with Japan seemed remote, even as the embers of conflict smoldered beneath the surface in the closing months of the year.

WINGS OF THEIR OWN

The sun hung low over the Gulf as Ensign Theodore "Teddy" Davidson walked across the tarmac at Pensacola one final time. His boots struck the concrete with a rhythm both proud and reluctant. Flight school was over. He had earned his wings. His white dress uniform, sharp and new, itched slightly at the collar, but the discomfort was lost beneath the gravity of the moment.

Top five in his class. That alone gave him options. And the Navy chose to assign him to Jacksonville Air Station for fighter training. The honor was dulled, however, by what awaited him there: the Brewster F2A Buffalo. Obsolete, overweight, and laughably sluggish compared to anything the Luftwaffe or the Japanese Zeroes could field. Pilots joked that the Buffalo could be outflown by a determined pigeon. But Teddy didn't complain. The truth was, he'd fly a barn door if it had an engine and wings. And besides, he'd heard that in Jacksonville, the training would soon shift to the Grumman F4F Wildcat—a stouter, deadlier fighter that could take a beating and bring you home.

Before his orders took effect, though, he had one precious week of shore leave. He spent it exactly where he wanted to: with Caroline, in Atlanta.

They rode the train north together, her hand folded over his, their elbows brushing with every sway of the car. Teddy talked. And talked. The thrill of takeoff, the pull of a hard banking turn, the shiver of turbulence. He rattled off aerial terms—aileron rolls, chandelles, Cuban eights—as if he were listing favorite songs. What he didn't mention was the unauthorized Immelmann he'd tried just days earlier, or how he'd stalled the aircraft and nearly spun out. That part stayed locked in the flight log of his own memory, a cautionary tale he wasn't quite ready to share.

Caroline laughed at his enthusiasm. She was beaming in her modest tan traveling dress, hair tucked back in a blue scarf, her blue eyes holding his with every smile. She told him she'd started her student teaching at a high school near her family home, and graduation was just around the corner.

They arrived in Atlanta to a warm dinner with her parents. Her father, Richard, was a tall, broad-shouldered man with a voice like rolled gravel and a handshake that lingered with meaning. Her mother, a petite woman named Irene, wore pearls at her neck and a quiet curiosity behind her eyes as she studied Teddy. The meal was fine Southern fare—roast chicken, greens, biscuits, and iced tea. Over dessert, Teddy leaned back and asked with a grin, "So, Caroline, what was this surprise you mentioned on the train?"

Her eyes sparkled mischievously. "I think I'll let Daddy explain," she said.

Her father chuckled. "Well, son, I've got a Stinson Reliant SR-10. Company plane. I use it to fly between our mills and plants across Georgia and the Carolinas. Caroline's been learning to fly her. And she's not half bad. Passed her first solo two months ago."

Teddy blinked, surprised and delighted. "You're a pilot?"

Caroline shrugged as though it were no big deal. "You inspired me. I figured if you could do loops and rolls, I could at least take off and land."

"Can we take her up, Dad?" she asked, nudging her father.

"Sure thing," he said, glancing out the window. "Still got enough daylight. She's fueled and ready to go."

Fifteen minutes later, they were driving down a narrow country road toward a small airstrip ringed by pecan trees and brush. The Stinson stood waiting on the edge of the field—sleek, high-winged, painted cream with navy trim and polished chrome accents that caught the setting sun.

Teddy stepped back and admired it. "She's a beauty."

"She is," Caroline said. "And tonight, she's mine."

She slipped into the front seat without hesitation, running through the pre-flight checks with practiced efficiency. Teddy climbed into the back, a little stunned but increasingly impressed. The open cockpit let the breeze drift through, stirring Caroline's hair as she started the engine and taxied to the edge of the grass runway.

With a calm hand on the throttle and another on the yoke, she launched them down the strip. The tail came up quickly, then the main wheels lifted. They were airborne.

She leveled off cleanly, eyes scanning the horizon. For a while they simply flew, the two of them passing control back and forth, trading jokes and marveling at the world below. Farms. Trees. Rivers shining like silver ribbons.

Teddy itched to try something—anything—but decided against showing off. Not yet. Not while she was still savoring her own control of the flight. But when they circled back toward the strip, he finally said, "Tighten your straps."

She glanced back. "Why?"

"I've got the controls."

He eased into a steady climb, then nudged the throttle forward. As the nose rose, he pulled back into a perfect loop. They soared upside down at the peak, the horizon spinning, then dipped back through the same path and leveled out.

When he handed back control, she was speechless for a moment. Then she laughed. "Daddy didn't teach me that one."

Teddy grinned. "You'll just have to enroll in Naval Flight School."

That night, they checked into a modest downtown hotel—quiet, elegant, with a dining room lit by candlelight and soft violin music in the corner. Their table was tucked in a private alcove, and every moment felt suspended, as though the war and the world were somewhere far off.

Over steak and wine, they talked about dreams. About flying. About what would happen if the world truly came undone. About what love meant when the future wasn't promised.

After dinner, they rode the elevator to their room, hands intertwined, shoulders brushing. Inside, the air was cool and still. Caroline unpinned her hair and let it fall over her shoulders.

Teddy cupped her face with one hand, brushing her lips with his. She responded gently at first, then urgently, her hands pulling him close. There was no hesitation now—no ceremony. Just two young lovers shedding layers of worry and formality.

Her dress slipped down, rustling to the carpet. His uniform jacket was gone in a flash, and his shirt followed. Skin met skin—warm, electric. They moved slowly at first, exploring, rediscovering. Her fingers traced the muscles of his back, his lips explored the soft line of her neck. He laid her down gently, reverently, and followed her into the quiet flame of passion.

They moved together with breathless grace, every touch a promise, every motion a vow. Their hearts pounded in unison, bodies entwined in perfect rhythm. He whispered her name; she moaned his. Time melted, leaving only sensation and sound and the unspoken bond that deepened with every passing second.

When it was over, they lay together in silence, her head on his chest, his arm draped around her shoulders.

The candlelight flickered across the ceiling like a far-off storm.

She broke the quiet. "You know what's funny?"

"What?"

"We still have separate bedrooms at my parents' house."

Teddy chuckled. "Do they really think—?"

"No," she said. "I'm sure they know. But appearances, right?"

He kissed her forehead. "We'll play our parts."

They returned to her parents' home late that night, slipping through the front door like schoolchildren returning past curfew. Her father met them in the hall and said nothing—just smiled knowingly and disappeared into the shadows.

Caroline padded off to her room. Teddy stood in the hallway for a moment longer, listening to the stillness of the house, before quietly stepping into the guest room.

He lay awake for a while, the scent of her hair still on his skin, the feel of her warmth still lingering like the last heat of a sunset.

Tomorrow, he would begin a new chapter. Jacksonville. The Brewster Buffalo. A war that seemed closer every day.

But tonight, he had wings of his own. And so did she.

He could only hope that soon, if luck and timing were kind, he'd be flying a Wildcat instead.

By the beginning of 1941, the United States Navy possessed seven aircraft carriers, five of which were deemed operational for wartime service. These carriers were actively deployed across the Atlantic and Pacific Oceans, tasked with ferrying aircraft to distant bases and conducting intensive training operations. A new generation of naval aviators was being shaped—young men learning to defy the laws of nature by launching from and landing on floating airstrips. Among these pilots, there was growing anticipation for the arrival of the Grumman F4F Wildcat, a rugged, faster replacement for the outclassed Brewster Buffalo. Though the Wildcat was far from perfect, its improved performance offered a glimmer of hope to those preparing for the mounting tensions on both oceans.

A MOTHER'S INTUITION

Having expressed his gratitude for their hospitality and said goodbye to Caroline's parents, Teddy stood beside the gleaming Yellow Lincoln waiting for a ride to the train station. The car caught his attention again, just as it had when they first pulled up a few days prior—its graceful lines, deep fenders, and that low-slung elegance that oozed power and refinement. He walked slowly around the car, lightly tapping its hood, marveling at the strength it seemed to radiate.

Inside the house, Caroline's mother was not ready to let her daughter go without a final word. In a tone that surprised even herself, and quite out of character, she cornered Caroline by the kitchen sink.

"Caroline," she said, her voice quiet but firm, "I

think you're making a mistake. You should be married by now—or at least engaged. You're giving yourself to someone without any promises, any security. This... this arrangement can't go on forever."

Caroline blinked in surprise. "Mother," she said softly, but with conviction, "Teddy and I have made our decision together. We don't need a ring to validate what we feel. We love each other, and I am perfectly happy waiting until the time is right. We both know what we want."

Just then, Caroline's father stepped into the kitchen. He had heard enough to understand the context and, as always, diffused the tension with his calm voice and reasoned tone.

"I think it's important," he said, looking gently at his wife, then his daughter, "that Teddy focuses on what's in front of him. He's about to learn how to take off and land on a moving aircraft carrier. There's no training more difficult for a pilot. Many will wash out. It'll take every bit of his skill—and his nerve. He doesn't need to worry about a wife just now."

It was rare to see her parents out of sync. Her mother's protective instincts clashed with her father's steady realism. But it was her dad's words that grounded Caroline again. She kissed him on the cheek, grabbed her coat, and rushed out the door.

Teddy looked up as she approached. "You're not smiling," he said, a little puzzled. "We've got time—we'll make the train."

Caroline shook her head. "It's not that. Let's go. I'll tell you on the way."

As they drove through downtown Atlanta toward the station, she told him about the kitchen confrontation. "Mother thinks we're making a mistake. That we're playing house without building one. It's the first time we've really argued. Dad stepped in and... well, he defended you. He said this next step in your life is going to take all your focus."

Teddy glanced at her, his brow furrowed. "I'm sorry you had to go through that. I never want to be the reason your mother feels anxious. I thought she liked me."

"She does," Caroline said. "She just doesn't like uncertainty. She wants the world locked up tight and promised in writing. But that's not the world we live in. And Dad's right. You've got enough on your plate without worrying about me. I'll be fine. I'll keep teaching. I'll write. I'll think of you."

Teddy reached over and gently squeezed her hand. "We'll get through this."

By the time they reached the platform, Caroline's mood had lightened again. The warmth had returned to her voice, and her smile widened.

"I don't want you leaving worrying about me and my parents," she said. "We're fine. I love you. And I believe in you."

They held each other for a long moment. Then Caroline pulled back slightly, locked eyes with him, and said, "Again, a kiss goodbye."

Their lips met with a fierce, passionate honesty that left no room for doubt or regret. Then, just like that, she turned away, walked down the platform, and did not look back.

Teddy stood watching until she disappeared into the crowd.

Jacksonville Naval Air Station was a sprawling hive of activity. Teddy arrived with a sea bag over his shoulder and hope in his chest. There was little ceremony to his reporting in—just a brief stop at the duty officer's desk and then a quick march to the office of his new commanding officer.

Lieutenant Commander John Swaggard, an aviator with twenty years' experience and a face like weathered leather, sat behind a desk reading Teddy's personnel file. His short-sleeved khaki shirt bore the sweat stains of a man who had long since stopped caring about appearances.

"You're too good to be true, Davidson," he said, scanning the sheet. "Top quarter of your class. Solid engineering background. Good marks from your instructors. And someone tells me you're also a decent guy. Can't have all four."

Teddy grinned. "I hope to not disappoint you, sir."

Swaggard stood and walked over to the window, hands behind his back.

"Plenty of good pilots don't make good carrier pilots," he said. "Flying off a field is one thing. Flying off a floating postage stamp that's pitching in three dimensions is something else. Judging your closure speed to a moving deck, dealing with crosswinds, deck turbulence, wake—takes a different breed. It's not just skill, it's perception. Nerve. Timing."

He turned to face Teddy directly. "We'll train you. And then we'll take you to sea."

Training at Jacksonville was grueling by design. Each day began at 0430 with muster, followed by a brisk calisthenics' routine on the tarmac—push-ups, jumping jacks, runs in formation, and sometimes a swim if the day's weather permitted.

By 0600, breakfast in the mess—powdered eggs, toast, coffee strong enough to wake the dead.

At 0700, classroom instruction began. Subjects included ship recognition, squadron tactics, gunnery theory, and the complex aerodynamics of carrier takeoffs and landings. Films of both successful and catastrophic carrier landings were shown to hammer home the stakes.

At 1000, they suited up and headed to the flight line. The aircraft assigned to Teddy and most of his classmates was the Brewster F2A Buffalo—a tubby, underpowered little beast that had already proven itself obsolete in the Pacific. Still, it was an aircraft, and it flew. Barely.

After pre-flight checks and coordination with ground crew, Teddy would taxi to the end of the runway, listening to the tower's commands through his headset. On takeoff, he pushed the throttle full forward, feeling the sluggish rumble as the Buffalo clawed its way into the air. Flying in pairs or threes, they practiced formation flying, dive bombing, mock dogfights, and approach patterns.

The most critical—and dreaded—part of the day came midafternoon: landing practice. Each cadet had to master a simulated carrier approach, using a painted outline on the airfield deck, and later, short field landings on barges and shortened strips. The Landing Signal Officer (LSO), known as the "paddles," stood at the far end of the strip, signaling with colored paddles. A proper landing required the pilot to hit a tight groove between stall speed and deck alignment, with less than a foot of vertical bounce.

On more than one occasion, Teddy caught a tongue-lashing from the LSO for "coming in hot" or "floating like a goose." But he learned. Day by day, he learned.

Evenings were for debriefing, lectures, and simulator time. Then study. Then, maybe, a letter written to Caroline before lights out at 2200.

After several weeks of intense training, Teddy began to shine. His takeoffs became smoother. His landings more precise. He earned the respect of Swaggard and even got a few dry compliments from the LSOs.

"I might just make a carrier pilot out of you yet," one instructor said, clapping him on the back.

One day, Swaggard summoned him to his office.

"We've pushed your group forward to Norfolk," he said. "You'll be boarding the Langley next week. She's not a war-fighter anymore, but she's still got her stripes. You'll get real deck time—real approaches, real launches. No more painted outlines."

Teddy nodded, the weight of the moment settling in. Carrier qualification. It was the final gate—and the hardest one yet.

Norfolk smelled like salt and oil. The docks teemed with supply crews, sailors in formation, and aircraft in crates being hoisted aboard ships bound for the Pacific. It was organized chaos—alive with the purpose of a nation preparing for war.

Teddy stood on the pier with a handful of fellow

aviators, looking up at the USS Langley. She looked tired. Once proud, now painted in dull gray with rust blooming along her seams. But her flat deck still stretched invitingly toward the open sea.

He took a breath.

"Again, a kiss goodbye," he whispered to himself, touching Caroline's latest letter in his breast pocket.

And then he walked aboard.

Throughout the summer of 1941, the front page news continued to be centered on activities in Europe. The war there was full on with continued success by the Germans. The back page news was the negotiations taking place between Japan and the United States over oil, mineral rights, and activities in the South Pacific where Japan had continued to expand its empire. On November 20, 1941, Japanese negotiators presented Washington with an ultimatum, basically threatening war if they weren't free to acquire the necessary rubber, oil, and minerals needed for their wartime economy.

LEARNING TO LAND

The light spray of saltwater curled into the wind as Ensign Theodore "Teddy" Davidson stood along the starboard catwalk of the USS Langley, eyes locked on the vast stretch of Atlantic sky. He had just completed his second practice carrier landing—barely sticking the deck —and though his legs still trembled beneath his crisp khaki uniform, he wore the grin of a man who had just outwitted gravity. Twice.

Landing on a carrier was a special kind of madness. The deck was a postage stamp in motion, and the moment of touchdown was either the end of a perfect equation or the beginning of disaster. Teddy had memorized every inch of the Langley's deck, but in motion, everything changed. The sea had a cruel way of reminding a man he was never really in control.

He wiped the sweat from his brow and glanced up at

the small control tower. Lieutenant Commander "Red" Haskins gave him a silent nod from the bridge window—approval, maybe even a touch of pride. Haskins didn't hand those out like candy.

Below deck, the narrow corridors smelled of grease, old coffee, and ambition. Teddy ducked under pipes and stepped over a coil of cable as he headed toward the ready room. Inside, a dozen young men sat in flight suits, a few with cigarettes dangling from tired mouths, others scribbling in their logbooks. The buzz of debriefings and low jokes filled the air like static.

"Davidson," barked Haskins as he entered behind him. "Not bad for a Kansas farm boy. You stuck the hook, but you drifted left on final. Cut that slop or the deck crew's going to pull you out of the drink next time."

"Yes, sir," Teddy said.

Haskins gave him a long look, then softened just slightly. "You've got the instincts. Clean it up and you'll be leading a flight by spring."

That meant something. Carrier landings were a crucible. You either walked away a pilot—or didn't walk away at all.

That evening, Teddy found a moment of quiet in the mess, stirring a bowl of overcooked stew. His hands still buzzed from the adrenaline. Across the table, Ensign Mike Tolland leaned back in his chair, humming a popular Glenn Miller tune off-key.

"You hear what the boys on the radio are saying?" Mike asked, picking up a piece of bread. "Japanese diplomats talking tough. Oil, rubber, territory in the Pacific. They want us to back off."

Teddy took a bite before answering. "They're already in Indochina. And we froze their assets this summer. Now they want negotiations."

Mike leaned forward. "Negotiations, my foot. They're stalling. You think we're going to end up in it?"

Teddy hesitated. "I think we're already in it. We just haven't said it out loud yet."

Mike nodded. "You ever wonder if we'll actually fire a shot before Christmas?"

Teddy looked at his spoon. "I don't know. But I think I'll be flying somewhere I've never heard of before long."

Back in his quarters, Teddy pulled out a worn envelope from under his pillow. Caroline's letter had already been read a dozen times, but each time felt like the first.

Dearest Teddy,

The trees are starting to turn in Atlanta—gold and scarlet. It reminds me of our walk after the mixer, the way you looked at me when you said the future made your heart race. I believe you now. I hear the future too, Teddy, and sometimes it scares me. But mostly it makes me proud. I tell anyone who'll listen that my sweetheart is flying off ships, doing something bigger than both of us.

Mother's growing impatient again. She says I should stop waiting and get married. But I keep telling her—this isn't about waiting. It's about loving someone enough to let them chase their calling.

Don't rush back for my sake. Just be careful. I want every part of you safe and whole when you return.

All my love,

Caroline

Teddy held the letter against his chest. She understood him in ways no one else could. Her words weren't perfume and fantasy—they were steel and silk. He didn't need to be across an ocean to feel how far apart they sometimes were, but her voice always brought him home.

He slid the letter back into its envelope and tucked it into the small locker beside his bunk. Outside, the engines of the Langley hummed a steady rhythm. He closed his eyes and tried to hold onto her voice in his mind.

Days passed quickly aboard ship. The routine hardened into ritual: morning flight drills, afternoon lectures on Japanese naval movements, and evenings filled with mechanical checks, map work, and the clatter of card games. Teddy trained in Brewster Buffalos—sturdy, underpowered relics by comparison to the Grumman Wildcats he hoped to get soon.

Still, he learned everything those planes could teach. He practiced barrel rolls, vertical reversals, formation loops. He trained not just to fly but to fight—wingtip to wingtip, trusting in his teammates, trusting in his own hands.

More than anything, he learned to listen. Listen to the wind, the engine, the feel of the stick as it whispered warnings. He made mistakes, but never twice. Red Haskins made sure of that.

One night, in the narrow glow of the navigation lamp, Teddy wrote a letter to Caroline. It was brief—his fingers were tired, and the ink kept skipping.

Caroline,

I'm starting to understand what this job means. It's not about flying tricks. It's about keeping people alive. And it's about not wasting time—time with you, time with the world before all this changes.

I think about you more than I admit, even to myself.

I'll be home again soon. And when I am, I want to dance with you in the street, like fools.

Love always,

Teddy

By late September, news was filtering in from the radio room with more urgency. Japanese fleet movements. Diplomatic backchannels growing tense. The Navy had ordered new defensive positions across the Pacific and East Coast alike. Teddy wasn't cleared for the intelligence, but the shift in posture was obvious.

That same week, the Langley anchored at Norfolk Naval Base for supplies. On the second day ashore, Teddy and Mike slipped out during leave to get real food at a small diner just outside the base perimeter.

It was the kind of place that served apple pie with a wink and called every sailor "hero." The booths were red vinyl, and the jukebox in the corner played Tommy Dorsey one moment and Hank Williams the next.

They sat over hot coffee and thick sandwiches. The waitress, barely twenty and smiling too much, left them alone once she saw the fatigue behind their eyes.

"I've got a girl in Charleston writing me every week," Mike said. "Swears she's going to wait for me. I don't believe her."

"You say that every time," Teddy replied.

"You believe in that stuff? Waiting? Love letters and promises?"

Teddy didn't answer right away. Then he said, "Yeah. I do."

Mike raised his cup in mock salute. "To true believers."

Back aboard ship in early October, training resumed at double pace. Rumors swirled—new fighters, new commands, even temporary stationing at Pearl. But for now, Teddy was exactly where he needed to be: in the air, preparing for a mission whose shape he could feel but not yet see.

That night, Haskins gathered the squadron in the ready room for a short address.

"Men, I don't have to tell you the world is shifting under our feet. We've had the luxury of preparation. But that luxury is nearly over. You'll be assigned squadrons soon. You'll be flying real missions, not just drills. And some of you will be sent farther west than you've ever been."

The silence in the room grew thick.

"Stay sharp. Watch each other's six. And remember why we're here. It's not glory. It's duty."

Later, Teddy stood alone near the railing, watching the harbor lights flicker along the dock. He thought about Kansas. About Caroline. About the wheat fields and the church bells and the fireflies of summer nights. It wasn't homesickness—it was focus. A reminder of what he was carrying with him.

A voice broke the stillness.

"You ever get tired of looking out like that?"

It was Haskins again, sipping coffee.

"No, sir," Teddy said. "Feels like I'm looking toward something."

Haskins nodded. "You are. Just don't forget to look back sometimes."

October 5, 1941

WHILE AMERICA BEGINS TO AWAKE

They returned to the hotel in the waning light, hands joined, the soft glow of street lamps following them down the corridor. Teddy unlocked the door to their room—a warm, modest space overlooking the Elizabeth River. A ship's horn sounded somewhere in the darkening distance. He set his cap on the bureau and turned toward her.

Caroline stepped into his arms as naturally as breathing, her lips brushing the line of his jaw. "Show me how you feel," she whispered. "No words. Not yet."

Their first kiss inside the room was slow, familiar, and deep—an unhurried blending of warmth and memory. Teddy's hands traced the shape of her back, finding their way down to her waist. He lifted her gently, and she let her shoes fall to the floor with a soft thump. When she reached for the buttons of her dress, he stopped her with a quiet smile.

"Let me."

He unfastened each button slowly, reverently, until her shoulders and the graceful lines he loved were revealed in the soft lamplight. She eased his shirt from his body, fingertips lingering on his chest before she leaned in to kiss his shoulder.

They settled onto the bed—side by side, then closer still—kissing, touching, letting the last of their day dissolve in the quiet heat between them. Clothes slipped away in a natural rhythm, familiar from the love they'd already shared, comfortable as breath.

What followed was not the urgency of their earlier days together, nor the exploratory passion of new lovers, but something quieter, deeper. They came together slowly, holding each other close, their movements deliberate and tender. It did not take long—neither needed it to. They knew each other too well, loved each other too much, for pretense or performance.

Caroline clung to him with a soft gasp, her body rising gently to his as the moment peaked and passed in a warm, shared wave. Teddy held her tightly, buried against her neck, whispering her name as the last tremors faded.

When it was over, they stayed fused, breathing softly against one another until their pulses slowed. Teddy rolled onto his back and Caroline curled against him, resting her cheek on his chest, their legs tangled beneath the sheets. He brushed a loose strand of hair from her forehead and kissed it.

For a long moment, the only sound was their breathing and the faint murmur of the river beyond the window.

Then Teddy exhaled a thoughtful breath.

"Can I ask you something?"

Caroline smiled without lifting her head. "Of course."

"I've always wondered... why you were standing directly behind me that night at the dance. You were close enough that I almost stepped on you."

She groaned softly and buried her face deeper against his chest. "Oh no. That's an embarrassing story. I was hoping you'd forgotten about that."

"Forgotten?" he laughed gently. "It was the moment everything changed for me. I've replayed it a hundred times. So yes—I want to hear it."

Caroline drew a slow breath, then shifted upward just enough to meet his eyes.

"All right," she said. "But just remember—you asked for this."

"I'm braced," he said, smiling.

She swatted his chest lightly, then began.

"My mother was a Tri-Delt. Delta Delta Delta. It was practically her religion. She always imagined I'd follow in her footsteps—pearls, charity teas, white dresses, the whole thing. The problem was, I didn't really see the point. During my freshman and sophomore years I barely paid attention to rush week. And because of that, even though I was a legacy, the sorority showed about as much interest in me as I showed in them.

"But by my junior year, some of my friends had joined Tri-Delt and begged me to at least go through rush week seriously—to give it an honest try. So, I did. And when I told my mother, she was so excited she nearly redecorated the living room in light blue."

He chuckled. "I can picture that."

"Well," Caroline continued, "they treated me differently because I was a junior—not as much hazing or ritual nonsense. But the girls saw an opportunity to tease me at that dance. You were there, this tall, handsome midshipman nobody had ever seen with a girl. So naturally, they came up with two theories. One: you didn't like girls. Or two: there was someone back home.

"They wanted to know the truth. And since I was the new prospective Tri-Delt, they put it to me: 'Caroline, you go ask him to dance.'"

"So that's why you were behind me," Teddy murmured.

"Yes," she said. "I was about to tap your shoulder and ask you to dance. And then you turned around, ran right into me, and asked me first—saving me completely from their little test. I think I nearly melted with relief."

She brushed her fingers across his cheek.

"And the rest," she whispered, "changed our lives. Forever."

Teddy smiled, full and quiet, pulling her closer.

"So," he murmured, "I suppose I owe a thank-you to Delta Delta Delta?"

She laughed softly into his chest. "We both do."

He kissed the top of her head, holding her for a long, contented moment.

On the morning of December 7th, 1941, the U.S. naval base at Pearl Harbor was ablaze after a surprise and devastating aerial assault by Japanese forces. Within two hours, over 2,400 Americans were dead, eight battleships were damaged or sunk, and hundreds of aircraft were destroyed on the ground. The Japanese, in contrast, suffered only minor losses, returning to their carriers with the confidence of a mission accomplished.

What seemed like a masterstroke of military planning was, to the American public, a betrayal of staggering proportions. No formal declaration of war had preceded the attack. Japanese diplomats were still engaged in talks with U.S. officials in Washington, creating a veneer of diplomacy while the attack was already underway. The sheer deceptiveness—and what many Americans perceived as the cowardice—of such tactics seared itself into the national psyche. The phrase "Remember Pearl Harbor" would become both a rallying cry and a vow of vengeance.

Fortune, however, played a role in limiting the scope of the disaster. None of the U.S. Navy's aircraft carriers were present at Pearl Harbor that day. All had been deployed at sea, either on training exercises or missions to deliver aircraft to distant outposts. Their survival would prove critical in the coming months as the Pacific war escalated.

In a swift and unexpected move, Adolf Hitler declared war on the United States just days later, aligning Nazi Germany with Japan and Italy in the Axis pact. With that declaration, America—still recovering from the shock of the Pacific attack—was now fully thrust into a global conflict. Whether it had sought war or not, the United

States was now at the center of a world war that spanned both oceans and continents.

DELIVERING BUFFALOS

The train platform in Norfolk was crowded but quiet, as if everyone there understood the gravity of the moment. Steam hissed from beneath the wheels, and the locomotive gave a long, low whistle. Theodore "Teddy" Davidson stood in his dress whites, a C-bag slung over one shoulder, a B-4 bag gripped in his hand. But neither felt heavy. All the weight in the world was in his chest, in the ache of the moment.

Caroline was in his arms, holding him so tightly he could feel the beat of her heart against his ribs. He could smell her hair—jasmine and summer rain. Her fingers gripped the back of his neck, and her voice, trembling with both love and fear, had barely spoken above a whisper since they'd arrived.

"I don't care how long the train ride is," she finally said, stepping back to look into his eyes. "I just care about this moment."

The conductor's final call echoed down the platform. Passengers bustled into line, voices raised, bags shifting, goodbyes becoming urgent. Teddy stayed still. He didn't want to move, didn't want to let go.

Then she looked up at him with that big, unforgettable smile and said, with a pause full of meaning:

"Again... a kiss goodbye."

And she kissed him—long, full, desperate, and

unashamed. Around them the world blurred away. When she finally pulled back, her eyes glistened withheld-back tears. She turned before he could see them fall and rushed into her father's waiting arms.

Teddy took one last look, lifted his bag, and stepped onto the train. He didn't look forward to the five-day journey. Not to the cramped seats or greasy food or endless stretches of track. And not to the emptiness he already felt growing with every mile.

The train ride west was every bit as tiresome as he'd imagined. He ate when he had to, slept when he could, and stared out the window at a country shifting from autumn leaves to western plains. By the fifth day, his uniform was rumpled, and his appetite had surrendered to the ever-present tang of canned beans and burned coffee. His heart raced with anticipation as the train slowed entering San Francisco.

The first thing he saw as he reached the docks was the towering gray profile of the USS Enterprise. She was massive, alive with movement and noise, sailors running lines, officers shouting orders, and planes being readied on deck. He felt small—and proud.

Reporting aboard, he found the duty officer, who nodded after checking the orders.

"Squadron Commander Trotter. You'll find him forward, Officer's Quarters. Welcome aboard, Lieutenant."

Teddy paused at the title but said nothing. He made his way through narrow steel corridors, bulkheads painted Navy gray, the scent of salt and oil and fresh paint all mingling in his nose. He knocked on the hatch marked VF-6 – Commander Frank Trotter.

"Enter," came the voice.

Teddy stepped in and stood at attention. "Theodore Davidson reporting for duty, sir."

Behind the desk sat a stocky man with close-cropped hair and sleeves rolled neatly above the elbows. Commander Frank Trotter looked up, sized him up, and smiled.

"That's Lieutenant Theodore Davidson," he said, setting down a pen. "Congratulations. Your commission came through while you were en route. We'll toast to it later."

Teddy allowed a brief smile. "Thank you, sir. That's very good news."

"Good. Because you'll be earning those bars right away. We're getting underway shortly."

Teddy straightened. "Where to, sir?"

Trotter leaned back in his chair. "You'll get full orders at sea. But I'll give you a hint—we've got a deck full of Brewster Buffalos. You didn't see any Wildcats out there, did you?"

"No, sir."

"They're in the hangar. Don't worry. But those Buffalos are on their way out—to Wake Island. God help the boys who end up flying them. Your assignment will be on the bulletin board outside. We're rotating top cover while the dive bombers and torpedo planes stay grounded. Limited fuel means we fly smart and sparingly. Got it?"

"Yes, sir."

"The petty officer outside will show you to your quarters. Get some chow, take a shower. You look like a man who's just traveled cross-country on government rails."

"I have, sir."

"Then rest up. Briefing at 0800 sharp."

Teddy saluted crisply. Trotter returned it with equal sharpness. "Dismissed."

By 0800 the next morning, Teddy had slept better than he expected, eaten real eggs, and even shaved. He felt more himself again. But he hadn't seen the ship pull away, hadn't glimpsed the Golden Gate Bridge or the skyline shrinking behind them. By the time he emerged for the morning briefing, they were well out to sea.

The ready room was packed with young officers, many still shaking off sleep. The scent of coffee filled the air. As Teddy entered, Commander Trotter stepped forward and raised a hand.

"Gentlemen," he said. "Before we begin—let's welcome our newest Lieutenant. Davidson, front and center."

Teddy stood, trying not to show surprise as the room erupted in applause. He made his way forward, where Trotter handed him a small box. Inside gleamed the silver bars of a Second Lieutenant.

"Sorry, there's no scotch on board," Trotter said. "But congratulations. You'll do well."

"Thank you, sir."

"Now, down to business."

He pulled down a wide map of the Pacific, marked with pins, lines, and coded notations. A low murmur passed through the room.

"This is where we are," Trotter said, pointing. "Our first stop is Pearl Harbor. We'll be there early December for refueling and reprovisioning. After that, we proceed directly to Wake Island to drop off the Buffalos."

A few groans passed quietly around the room.

"I know," Trotter added. "Those planes are outdated. But it's not our place to argue. While aboard, our top cover flights will rotate daily. That means you, gentlemen. Fly clean, fly smart, and don't show off. We're operating with a crowded deck and no room for mistakes. Flights only go up in good weather and under favorable winds. Until we unload those Buffalos, we're running tight."

He nodded toward the side wall. "Your assignments are posted on the bulletin board. If your name's not up, you're backup. Questions?"

None.

"Good. Dismissed."

Four days later, Enterprise docked at Pearl Harbor. Fuel lines were connected, crates were unloaded, and sailors fanned out into the city with 48-hour passes. Teddy stood at the rail and stared at the shoreline. He knew the stay would be short—but he also knew the feeling in his gut. He was on the edge of something.

The world was shifting. The Pacific was growing tense. And for all the training, for all the hours in the air, he could feel it—the unmistakable hum of war rising with the tide.

That evening, Teddy joined a few of his fellow pilots and headed into Honolulu. The city buzzed with music and voices, sailors weaving through bars and clubs like they didn't have a care in the world. Teddy had a couple of beers, laughed with the others, but he wasn't much of a drinker, and the noise made him restless.

Later, he broke off on his own and walked down to the beach. The moonlit surf rolled quietly against the shore, and Diamond Head rose like a dark sentinel at the far end of the bay. He stood barefoot in the sand, hands in his pockets, staring out over the water and thinking of Caroline. The sound of the waves and the feel of the tropical breeze made him think how perfect it would be if she were here. He imagined walking this beach with her, her hand in his, her laughter echoing across the water.

Before returning to the ship, Teddy's last mission on land was to find postcards. He bought a stack and sat down at a cafe table, scribbling out notes. One for his family. One for Coach Leland back at the high school. And of course, one for Caroline. He didn't say too much —just that the place was beautiful, that he was safe, and that he missed her more than anything.

He assumed he'd be back here soon. Pearl Harbor was where they'd likely be stationed after their run to Wake Island. It felt certain, almost obvious. He imagined meeting Caroline here one day, watching her eyes light up as she took in the beauty of the islands.

Two days later, with shore leave complete and provisions loaded, the *Enterprise* set a course west. Upon arrival at Wake Island, the deck crew began unloading the

Brewster Buffalos in the sweltering heat. The pilots stood back, helmets tucked under arms, wondering what kind of future these old birds had.

Then came the news. Word filtered through the ranks slowly at first, like a rumor too wild to be true.

Pearl Harbor had been attacked.

The Battle of the Coral Sea, fought in early May 1942, marked a pivotal turning point in the Pacific War. Although tactically inconclusive—with both the United States and Japan suffering significant losses—the battle was a strategic victory for the Allies. Most importantly, it halted the Japanese southward advance and prevented what appeared to be an imminent invasion of Australia.

Each side lost a major aircraft carrier: the Japanese light carrier Shōhō was sunk, while the American carrier Lexington was lost. The fleet carrier Shōkaku sustained serious damage, and several other vessels on both sides were crippled. Yet it was not just the loss of steel and ships that defined the cost—it was the loss of experienced pilots.

For Japan, these losses were far more devastating. Unlike the United States, which had the industrial capacity and training programs to replenish its ranks, Japan's seasoned naval aviators were irreplaceable. Their training regimen had been long and elite, but not scalable. The death of a pilot was not just a human loss—it meant a permanent reduction in future capability.

For the first time, the Japanese advance had been stopped. And for the first time in history, a major naval battle had been waged entirely by aircraft launched from carriers. The ships themselves never came within sight of one another. The Coral Sea had proven that the aircraft carrier—not the battleship—was now the king of naval warfare. most of the news from the war was bad. The Philippines were falling, and General MacArthur had to be smuggled out by PT boat under the cover of night, eventually reaching safety in Australia.

A BUMP ON THE HEAD

Teddy Davidson rose slowly, as if coming up from a deep darkness. Light came first—harsh and white—followed by a vague pressure behind his eyes. Somewhere nearby, a voice spoke his name. He tried to answer, but the words lagged behind his thoughts. A shape leaned closer, resolving into a face, and then a hand holding a small flashlight.

"Follow the light for me, Lieutenant."

The beam moved back and forth. Teddy complied, blinking, his head throbbing dully. His last clear memory was fractured—flying reconnaissance and extended top cover, the sudden slash of silver in the sun, Japanese Zeros dropping out of altitude like hawks. Gunfire. Smoke. The violent shudder of his Wildcat. Then the deck of the Enterprise rushing up far too fast, steel filling his windscreen as he crash-landed what remained of his aircraft and lost consciousness.

"You with me, son?" the medical officer asked. "How many fingers am I holding up?"

Teddy squinted. "Three, sir."

"That's right. And can you tell me where you are?"

Teddy hesitated, his mind still crowded with images that didn't belong to the present—Kansas fields bending under the wind, Georgia Tech classrooms, Caroline's laugh, flight training, the long blue wake of the Pacific stretching endlessly behind a carrier deck. All of it had replayed in his head in what felt like hours, though he knew it could only have been minutes.

"Well," he said carefully, "I'm pretty sure I'm not in Kansas."

A ripple of laughter moved through the small medical compartment. Teddy smiled faintly, reassured by the sound. He took a breath, steadier now. "I crash-landed my Wildcat," he added. "On the Enterprise. Took a hit to the head."

The doctor nodded, satisfied. "That you did. A solid bump, but nothing that looks permanent. Take it easy for a bit—though I suspect that won't last long. You tangled with the enemy less than ten miles north of us."

Teddy swung his legs over the edge of the bunk and stood. His head protested, but his balance held. "Thank you, sir."

Minutes later, back in his bunk space, he pulled on a fresh flight suit and considered lying down. Instead, he headed for the ready room. Whatever the headache, the war was awake now—and so was he.

Teddy was asleep in the ready room when the blaring alarm jolted him upright.

"All hands! General Quarters! General Quarters!"

He was already half-suited, his gear nearby, when Lieutenant Commander Trotter entered briskly.

"Good, you're ready to go. We need you to man your planes. Here's the situation—your division will accompany bombers and torpedo bombers. Your job is to protect them and protect yourselves. Altitude is your advantage. Use hit-and-run tactics. Do not get into a dogfight. Understood?"

He pointed to the chalkboard map behind him. "These are your coordinates. The bombers and torpedo bombers launch first. You'll take off last, climb above them, and escort them in. Once their run is done, our top cover will come down to refuel and then rotate back up. Any questions? No? Good luck."

Teddy's heart pounded—not with fear, but focus. He had earned flight leader status, though not full squadron command. He turned to the three other pilots in his flight.

"Let's stay tight. If we get separated, climb to altitude and regroup. We've got a long road ahead with these Japanese pilots, but it won't all be settled today. Conserve fuel. Learn what you can. Let's get back safely."

One by one, they climbed into their Wildcats, buckled in, and waited. First the bombers. Then the torpedo bombers. Then the signal. The deck crew gave the thumbs-up, and the Wildcats roared forward, joining the growing formation headed toward battle.

Teddy was first to spot the aircraft carriers and their Japanese fleet. He pivoted his head quickly, repositioning the scarf that he had worn since childhood—once sentimental, now necessary. The constant scanning of the sky, checking for enemy fighters, could quickly rub your neck raw without it. The scarf shielded him from that, padding his flight jacket's collar. Tradition or not, it served a real purpose.

"Stay off the radio unless you've got something important to report," Teddy instructed.

Below them, the formation of Kates shimmered like a school of fish, their silver wings catching flecks of morning sun as they leveled out into an attack run. Teddy steadied his breathing and eased the throttle forward, feeling the Wildcat respond with a familiar vibration. He selected the closest Kate, sighting ahead of its nose.

He fired. The six .50-caliber machine guns roared, streaks of white tracers striking the engine cowling. The Kate jerked violently, broke apart, and spiraled into the sea.

He spotted another Kate breaking formation and rolled left, matching its descending arc. The Japanese pilot tried to skim above the waves, hoping Teddy would overshoot. Instead, Teddy anticipated the movement and fired a long burst. The bomber erupted in a fireball, its torpedo detonating as it hit the water.

Before he regained altitude, a Zero dove from Teddy's high right, cannons blazing. Rounds tore across his right wing root, rattling the frame.

Teddy dove—hard.

The Wildcat screamed through the air at 260 knots. The Zero followed but hesitated, unwilling to overstress its lighter frame. Teddy pulled up at the last moment, converting his dive into a sweeping escape path. The Zero overshot.

He rolled hard right, climbing beneath the Zero's underside. The Japanese pilot turned vertically into an Immelmann, trying to regain altitude. Teddy anticipated it, climbing just enough to force a head-on threat. The Zero broke left, losing energy.

Teddy lined up and fired. Tracers erupted across the Zero's tail rudder, tearing fabric loose. The Japanese fighter broke away into the haze.

His right wing vibrated violently now—a panel

beneath the landing gear flapped loose. He tested his roll response: sluggish, but controllable.

Two of his wingmen rejoined him. The fourth was missing.

"You guys okay?" Teddy asked.

"We're fine," came the reply. "But you're trailing metal under your right wing."

Teddy exhaled. "All right then. Let's see if we can get this Cat home. Stay with me, guys.

By May of 1942, the U.S. Navy's carrier force was still developing, a small collection of ships carrying an outsized share of the nation's hopes in the early Pacific War. The Enterprise had already begun to distinguish herself through constant patrols, rapid deployments, and air groups gaining hard-earned experience. Her pilots were learning lessons that no training syllabus had ever anticipated—lessons written in exhaust trails, bullet holes, and narrow escapes over vast stretches of ocean. Each mission underscored the precarious reality of America's early war footing: every carrier mattered, every pilot mattered, and there were no reserves waiting in the wings.

The loss of the Lexington during the Coral Sea operations delivered a painful reminder of that vulnerability. "Lady Lex," one of the Navy's earliest and most beloved carriers, suffered catastrophic internal damage after sustaining multiple enemy hits. Though her crew fought with extraordinary discipline to contain the fires and keep her afloat, the decision was ultimately made to abandon and scuttle her. The sinking marked a turning point in the hearts of the men who served on America's remaining carriers. For aviators on ships like the Enterprise, the memory of the Lexington was ever-present—a symbol of the dangers they faced and a testament to the courage required to keep the Pacific from slipping entirely into enemy hands.

OVERBOARD

Teddy and his wingmen approached the American fleet, flying low over the ocean's choppy surface. The sky was tinged with haze and smoke. Thick black plumes curled skyward from multiple ships. One of them—the carrier Lexington—was belching smoke at a terrifying rate, and even from this distance, Teddy could see the scorch marks along its decks.

His Wildcat groaned as it banked, the airframe shuddering under stress. He keyed the radio. "Enterprise control, this is Davidson. Plane is damaged but flying. Fuel level green. Requesting landing instructions."

"Enterprise to Davidson. Circle. Priority to low-fuel aircraft. Confirm your condition."

"Copy. Will circle. Structural damage, unknown extent," Teddy replied, glancing at the twitching altimeter and the slight pull to the left in his controls.

He had survived his second battle. That much was clear. What wasn't clear—what no one yet could know— was who had won. Below, fire crews swarmed the deck of the Lexington, trying to contain damage that looked more serious than hopeful. Several destroyers maneuvered nearby, towing smaller craft and scanning the waves for survivors and debris.

Teddy's eyes scanned the horizon. His mind, however, was elsewhere—on his flight group. One plane was missing. He could account for only two of his wingmen. No parachute flares. No distress calls. Just silence. That silence, more than any damage to his own plane, haunted him as he circled.

Eventually, word came over the comms. "Enterprise to all damaged aircraft, you are cleared for landing. Prepare for reversed approach: stern to bow. Flight deck has been cleared. Approach carefully."

Teddy narrowed his eyes. A stern-to-bow landing was

unconventional, but it made sense. The ship's forward motion into the wind could help compensate for the lack of braking and shorten the effective stall speed. It was a lifesaver for pilots like him who weren't sure their gear would even hold.

As he began his descent pattern, Teddy toggled the landing gear switch. A deep metallic clunk sounded—but only one side locked. The other remained stubbornly retracted. He toggled again. No change. He looked out the canopy: the right gear hadn't deployed.

A cold certainty sank into his gut. He wasn't going to land this thing on wheels.

"Enterprise, Davidson again. Landing gear is only partially deployed. Right gear stuck. Request permission for belly landing."

A pause.

"Davidson, we copy. Permission granted. Deck is clear. Hangar secured. Top cover on standby. Proceed with extreme caution."

"Understood," Teddy said quietly. He pulled in a long breath, the leather of his gloves creaking as he tightened his grip on the stick. The Wildcat was a tough bird—he just hoped it was tough enough.

He made one final circle, dropping altitude. Full flaps. Airspeed: 75 knots. He trimmed for a glide, feeling the nose dip. The carrier loomed ahead, its massive form carving a path through the waves. Wind buffeted his plane. He felt it lift slightly—just as planned.

"Come on, baby," he whispered. "Hold together."

The belly of the Wildcat hit the steel deck with a shriek of metal on metal. Sparks exploded beneath him.

The entire plane lurched and skidded violently. With no arrestor hook and no landing gear, there was nothing to stop the forward momentum.

"Too fast," Teddy muttered, trying to use the rudder for any resistance. It didn't matter.

The Wildcat slid forward—straight off the edge of the deck.

The moment it happened, time seemed to slow.

Teddy felt a moment of eerie quiet, then a gut-wrenching drop as the plane left the deck and nosed over into the sea.

He braced. Impact.

The ocean swallowed him.

His helmet slammed against the canopy. Water burst through the seams, relentless. Disoriented, he gasped before realizing what he'd done—panic inhalation. His lungs burned. The cockpit was filling rapidly.

Instinct took over. He tore at the harness, fought off the parachute straps, and reached for the emergency lever. The cockpit canopy stuck. He slammed it with his elbow. Once, twice—then it slid open.

Above him, the sky was gone. Only the blurred shadow of the Enterprise loomed—growing larger.

The propellers.

That's when he understood.

The carrier had turned toward him. Not away. Toward.

The helmsman was trying to steer the massive ship over the wreckage—so the props wouldn't hit him.

It was both terrifying and brilliant.

Teddy pushed himself out of the cockpit. Water resistance slowed everything, but adrenaline surged. He kicked hard, feeling the sucking force of the Wildcat as it sank beneath him.

The carrier passed overhead. A dark metal ceiling.

Then, light—greenish and faint. He rose with what breath he had left. His Mae West vest inflated with a sharp tug, propelling him upward.

He broke the surface with a violent gasp, coughing and spitting salt water. The Enterprise's stern receded behind him.

Then he saw the destroyer.

"Pilot in the water!" someone shouted.

A rope ladder was thrown over the side, splashing near him. Moments later, strong arms reached down. Sailors in soaked helmets and grimy uniforms hauled him up, seaweed and oil trailing from his flight gear.

"Lieutenant Davidson?" one shouted over the chaos.

"That's me," Teddy rasped.

"Jesus. We thought you were chopped meat. You went under her bow!"

Teddy collapsed to his knees on the deck, coughing seawater and oil. He was shaking—not from fear, but from the sudden come-down after raw survival.

He was alive.

He had survived the Battle of the Coral Sea—and a belly landing gone wrong.

Aboard the destroyer USS Anderson, the ship's medical officer—a short, wiry man named Lieutenant Garvey—met him just inside the passageway.

"Get him below," Garvey barked. "I want him dry and horizontal."

Teddy barely protested as they guided him down into sickbay. His flight suit was soaked and reeked of salt, oil, and sweat. Garvey began peeling it away, inspecting his limbs, torso, and face.

"Big knot forming on your forehead," he muttered, shining a small penlight into Teddy's eyes. "Concussed, maybe. Pupils responsive. You're lucky. We've seen worse."

Teddy winced as the doctor poked his ribs. "Some bruising. Deep contusions down the left thigh and shoulder. Nothing broken. How's your vision?"

"Clear," Teddy croaked.

"Ears ringing?"

"A little."

Garvey nodded. "Rest. Fluids. You're grounded for a while, Lieutenant. Take it seriously."

Teddy managed a tired grin, eyes fluttering closed.

He drifted in and out of sleep over the next two days. The pain came and went. Headaches pulsed behind his eyes. But by the third morning, he was sitting up, hungry, and restless.

Three days later, the transfer boat eased alongside the Enterprise. Teddy climbed aboard slowly, legs still stiff and bandaged from bruises, but strength returning. The sun was out, the air smelled like ocean and salt and fuel. A few sailors on the hangar deck turned to look.

When he stepped off the boat and back onto the deck, a cheer erupted.

Pilots—some battered, some tired, all changed— gathered to meet him. Laughing. Slapping him on the back. Someone handed him a dry towel. Another tossed him a chocolate bar.

He grinned, wiping the salt from his face.

"Hell of a landing," someone said.

"I was aiming for the admiral's chair," Teddy shot back.

They laughed. They needed to laugh.

That night, they shared a modest celebration in the ready room—warm coffee, jokes, and a rare surprise from the galley: fried chicken, hot and crispy, the kind that made you forget where you were for just a moment.

Teddy's squadron leader raised a toast: "To the pilot who crashed his plane this morning, then belly-landed his second plane, then sank his bird, and swam with the sharks just to get back here—welcome home, Davidson."

The room echoed with cheers.

In the days that followed, word filtered through from command. The Lexington was gone. The Shōhō had been sunk. Shōkaku had taken damage. The Japanese advance toward Port Moresby had been halted. Strategically, it was a victory.

No one here felt like a winner.

But Teddy was alive. And so were most of his friends. They had learned. They had fought. They had become men.

And the war had only just begun.

By *late 1942, the demand for trained military pilots was at its peak, and women stepped forward to fill a vital gap in aviation logistics. In September of that year, the United States established the Women's Auxiliary Ferrying Squadron (WAFS), a pioneering group of female pilots tasked with ferrying aircraft from factories to military bases, thereby freeing up male pilots for combat duty. The WAFS would later merge with the Women's Flying Training Detachment to form the Women's Airforce Service Pilots (WASP), who flew nearly every type of military aircraft—without ever seeing combat themselves.*

Britain, too, employed women pilots in non-combat roles through the Air Transport Auxiliary, which saw women flying Spitfires, Hurricanes, and other warplanes to frontline units. Perhaps most remarkably, the Soviet Union deployed women in fully combatant roles, including the infamous "Night Witches" of the 588th Night Bomber Regiment and the all-female fighter units who flew Yak and LaGG aircraft against the Luftwaffe. While often overlooked in postwar narratives, these brave women proved themselves equal to the challenge of flight, danger, and duty.

BECOMING A W.A.S.P.

News reports of the Battle of the Coral Sea were slowly trickling back to the United States. Caroline, fully aware that Teddy was serving onboard the *Enterprise*, could not wait to get to the movie theater to watch the newsreels. She went every day, and every day a little bit more information was revealed to the American public. Caroline felt so much closer to Teddy just seeing the videos.

The American people were just coming to realize that, for the first time, the Japanese encroachment in the South Pacific had been stopped. It had come at a high price. And for Caroline, she was relieved that it had not come at a personal price—to her, or to his family.

The *Enterprise* steamed back toward Pearl Harbor along with the fleet. Many ships had taken damage and were in urgent need of repair. On the horizon loomed another confrontation—one that naval planners could sense but not yet define: the Battle of Midway.

Naval intelligence had, for some time, suspected a major attack on a U.S. base somewhere in the Pacific. But the details—where, when, and how—remained elusive. In the meantime, all the fleet could do was patch its wounds, replace lost planes and pilots, and prepare for what was coming. None of them knew then that the next battle would become a pivotal turn in the war.

Behind the scenes, however, in a secure facility at Pearl Harbor known as Station HYPO, a team of code-breakers led by Commander Joseph Rochefort had been working tirelessly to decrypt Japanese naval codes—specifically the JN-25 code used by the Imperial Japanese Navy. Fragments of intercepted communications hinted at a major operation codenamed "AF," but the question remained: what exactly was "AF"?

To test their theory, Rochefort and his team devised a clever ruse. Midway Island's base commander was instructed to send an unencrypted radio message stating that their water purification system had failed. Just days later, Japanese communications—still encoded, but partially readable—reported that "AF" was low on fresh water. It was the confirmation Rochefort needed. "AF" was Midway.

Admiral Chester W. Nimitz, Commander in Chief of the Pacific Fleet, trusted Rochefort's assessment. It was a bold decision, one that required immense confidence in intelligence rather than visible enemy movement. Acting on Rochefort's decrypted information, Nimitz ordered the carriers *Enterprise*, *Hornet*, and the hastily repaired *Yorktown* to take up a position northeast of Midway. The goal was to lie in wait—hidden from enemy reconnaissance—until the Japanese fleet approached.

The gamble was immense. Nimitz was placing his limited carrier force in harm's way based largely on code-breaking and educated guesses. But the timing, the positioning, and the reliance on America's still-young signals intelligence program would prove decisive.

And after that battle, there would be no looking back. The tide would begin to turn, slowly but unmistakably. The Japanese would find themselves on the defensive, forced to yield ground in a long and bloody campaign they had never anticipated.

Back in Atlanta, there was a news release recruiting women pilots to join the Women's Auxiliary Ferrying Squadron. Caroline jumped at the opportunity to make a contribution to the war effort. Recently graduated, and now with quite a few hours in her logbook, she was a very able pilot—one found very attractive by the military.

Admittedly, she told her parents that it was her

chance to get closer to the West Coast, as she would be ferrying planes from manufacturing facilities around the country to both coasts. She, no doubt, would be able to prioritize her assignments to the West Coast, always holding out the hope of seeing Teddy—even if just in passing.

Her training was to begin immediately. The demand was great, and the military made it clear: the war effort could not wait. Once deemed qualified and proficient, Caroline would be flying aircraft vital to the defense of the nation—freeing up male pilots for combat duty overseas and writing her own chapter in the history of American aviation.

The Battle of Midway, fought in June 1942, marked a decisive turning point in the Pacific War. Just six months after Pearl Harbor, the U.S. Navy—armed with broken Japanese codes—ambushed the overconfident Imperial fleet. Four Japanese carriers were sunk, dealing a crippling blow to their naval air power. The U.S. lost the Yorktown and a destroyer but preserved its core striking force.

Though the Coral Sea a month earlier was the first naval battle where opposing ships never saw each other, Midway delivered the more decisive outcome. It halted Japanese expansion and shifted the strategic initiative to the United States. From that point on, Japan would fight a defensive war.

The opening rounds for the battle at Midway were chaotic. American torpedo bombers attacked without fighter cover. US bombing squadrons became lost and unable to find the enemy. Meanwhile, Teddy's squadron engaged Japanese Zeros until their fuel was exhausted, then returned to the Enterprise.

ACE

Teddy grabbed a hot cup of coffee and a thick sandwich from the mess on his way to the ready room. The ship hummed with a barely contained tension—the kind that comes before the second act of a battle. The scent of burnt fuel and cordite still clung to his uniform. As he stepped into the ready room, the air was thick with sweat and chatter, pilots comparing notes, reliving kills, mourning losses.

An officer from intelligence called the room to order and delivered a brisk briefing. "Gentlemen, in thirty minutes, you're going back up. This time, you're flying top cover. Enemy counterattack expected. We need to keep our decks safe."

Teddy leaned forward. The officer continued, "You're credited with one and a half confirmed kills, Lieutenant Davidson. That brings your tally to three and a half."

There was no time for back-pats or celebration. Teddy asked immediately, "My flight?"

"All intact," the officer nodded, then looked down. "Torpedo Squadron Eight didn't come back. Not a single plane. But our dive bombers did a number on them. Three carriers hit."

A silence fell across the room, a quiet reverence for the torpedo men. Teddy had seen some of their planes limping back earlier, fuel spilling, flames trailing. Apparently, none had made it. He swallowed hard and nodded. The fight was over for them.

War was always fragmented—like watching a film through a keyhole. Pilots fought battles within battles, with no idea how their role fit into the whole. Even when victories occurred, the why or how didn't reach the cockpit.

Teddy finished his coffee. His body was tired, but he felt alive. Clear. Focused. He walked to the flight deck and gave his Wildcat a thorough inspection. She was dusty from gunfire residue, scratched along the fuselage, but she was intact. His hands moved along the cowling with respect. He checked the tail wheel, the flaps, the guns. Everything had held.

He strapped in, the cockpit closing over him like armor. His leather gloves creaked as he adjusted the throttle. The plane smelled of oil, gunpowder, and sweat. He checked his instruments—fuel, oil pressure, manifold pressure, artificial horizon, altimeter. All green.

His oxygen mask was slung over his face as he taxied into position. The deck crew signaled, and Teddy pushed the throttle forward, feeling the Wildcat leap ahead under its own power. The vibration smoothed into a steady hum as he climbed.

At 10,000 feet, he felt the chill through his jacket. At 15,000 feet, his breath condensed in his mask. The Pacific stretched below like a shimmering sheet, interrupted only by the wakes of the fleet and the dark scars of battle.

They formed a protective circle above the task force. The fleet looked small from this height, but Teddy could make out the Enterprise, the Hornet, and the destroyers in their screening pattern. He scanned constantly—sky, sea, gauges, his wingmen. A pilot's life depended on perpetual awareness.

Then the call came over the radio. "Bandits. Eleven o'clock low. Approaching fast."

Teddy and his flight dove. Below, he saw the enemy formation—a dozen Japanese torpedo bombers, Naka-jima B5Ns, coming in low, hugging the sea. Above them, a few Zero fighters flanked the bombers. The Japanese were betting on a low, fast strike.

Teddy's wingman radioed, "I'm on your six, Teddy. Let's clean 'em up."

Teddy pushed the stick forward, diving in a sweeping arc toward the formation. His eyes locked on the lead bomber. As he closed the gap, the Wildcat's guns chattered to life, the cockpit vibrating with the brutal rhythm. Tracers stitched the sky ahead of him, striking the tail of the bomber.

The Japanese aircraft burst into smoke and flame, spiraling into the water.

Teddy pulled up, rolled, then dived again. Another torpedo bomber tried to bank away, but Teddy was on him. He lined up the shot—steady, steady—and fired. This one erupted midair, debris splashing into the sea.

"Tally two," he breathed.

Now he pulled off and slid into wingman position. "Your turn, Duke," he said to his flight mate.

Duke dove hard and chased down a third bomber. His first pass missed, but on the second, he clipped the engine and the bomber went nose-first into the waves.

The fight wasn't over yet. Zeros broke through the top cover and tangled with the Wildcats. Teddy went evasive, spinning and diving as one Zero latched onto him. His Wildcat, though slower, was rugged. He bobbed and weaved, ducked behind Duke, and his wingman drove the Zero off.

"Stay tight," Teddy called.

Below, Japanese torpedo bombers kept coming. Some got through. The Hornet was hit—Teddy saw the smoke rise from her deck. His gut twisted, but he couldn't focus on that. Another bomber zoomed past, low and fast. He turned to follow, but it was too far gone.

They circled back, scanning for more threats. None remained.

Teddy's flight was intact. Low on ammo, he called in to return. The Enterprise welcomed them with a clear deck. One by one, they landed. Teddy's tires screeched across the deck as he braked, the tailhook catching with a jolt.

Back inside, he unzipped his flight jacket and peeled off his gloves. The room was buzzing. Someone handed him a debrief sheet. Another pilot slapped him on the back. Then the intelligence officer raised a hand and spoke above the din.

"Lieutenant Davidson. Your final count for today—two more confirmed. That brings you to five and a half kills."

A beat of silence—and then the ready room erupted in cheers.

"Hot damn, he's an ace!"

"First ace in the squadron!"

"Teddy, drinks on you in Honolulu!"

He was swarmed. Claps on the back, shoulders shaken, jokes flying. Someone tossed him a pair of gold-painted toy wings. Laughter echoed off the bulkheads. It wasn't just pride—they needed this. Something to celebrate. A break from the tension, from the death.

Teddy smiled, red-faced but honored. He knew what it meant—not just for him, but for every pilot there. He represented what was possible. What could be survived. What could be won.

Later, after the excitement faded and the pilots began to rest, a quiet announcement came over the PA system.

"The Enterprise and Task Force 16 will return to Pearl Harbor for resupply and repairs. Course set."

The fleet was victorious. Midway was behind them.

And ahead—Hawaii. Home soil. For a little while, at least.

FUEL
AIRSPEED
RPM
OILS
ATACK
RP 15
FIRE EXTD
GUNS
NAV

"At one stroke, the dominant position of Japan in the Pacific was reversed," British Prime Minister Winston Churchill wrote in his post-war account of World War II.

"The annals of war at sea present no more intense, heart-shaking shock than this battle, ... in which the qualities of the United States Navy and Air Force and of the American race shone forth in splendor."

President Franklin D. Roosevelt also honored the valor of those who fought at Midway, particularly Lieutenant John James Powers:

"He led [his squadron] down to the target from an altitude of 18,000 feet, through a wall of bursting anti-aircraft shells and swarms of enemy planes. He dived almost to the very deck of the enemy carrier and did not release his bomb until he was sure of a direct hit.... He had made good his promise to 'lay it on the flight deck.'"

LIFE IN THE COCKPIT

Teddy lay in his bunk aboard the carrier, one arm across his forehead, half-asleep but wide awake in his mind. The memory returned unbidden, vivid and immersive—his senses reliving every moment of the fight, as if he were still there, strapped into the cockpit of his Grumman F4F Wildcat, battling a Mitsubishi A6M Zero in the skies over the Pacific in 1942.

It had been a visceral blend of tension, sensory overload, and split-second decision-making, pitting man and machine against one of the most feared fighters of the war.

The Wildcat's cockpit was a tight, utilitarian space. He remembered being wedged into a narrow seat, harness biting into his shoulders, a parachute strapped to his back and the added bulk of a life vest pressing against him. The canopy framed the sky, offering visibility ahead and to the sides, but leaving dangerous blind spots below and behind. He'd been hyper-aware, constantly scanning. Instruments surrounded him—altimeter, airspeed indicator, fuel gauge, manifold pressure, RPM—each a silent sentinel demanding attention. The throttle and control stick had been close at hand, the gunsight poised above the dash, six .50-caliber Brownings, aligned and waiting.

The air smelled of rubber from his oxygen mask, mixed with sweat and the faint tang of aviation fuel. The deep roar of the Pratt & Whitney radial engine had vibrated through the cockpit and into his chest, a living, pounding heartbeat. Even through the headset, the engine's thunder had been relentless, broken only by the urgent chatter of his squadron over the radio. His every movement felt exaggerated in that tight space, adrenaline sharpening every nerve.

He'd caught a glint of sunlight off a canopy ahead—a Zero. Sleek, deadly, fast. It could out-turn and out-climb him with ease. It had always reminded him of a blade—thin, agile, a predator in the sky. But his Wildcat had strengths the Zero didn't. Armor behind the seat. Self-sealing tanks. Durability. If it came to a slugfest, he could absorb punishment and keep fighting. The Zero could not.

It had come at him hard, banking for a rear position. His response had been automatic—throttle forward, nose down. The Wildcat dove like a rock with a tailfin, picking up speed past 300 knots. The ocean blurred. The altimeter spun. G-forces flattened him in the seat as he yanked back on the stick at 2,000 feet. The Wildcat groaned, and blood drained from his head as the horizon curved.

The Zero stayed glued to him. He'd seen it flick and jink, trying to line up a shot. Tracers sizzled past his canopy—crackling streaks of death that missed by inches. His heart had pounded harder than the engine.

He couldn't play the Zero's game. A turning fight was suicide, and climbing was no better—the Zero could out-climb him easily. But he could make it think he was climbing.

He rolled hard right into a steep ascent, watching through the canopy as the Zero responded, following. At the peak of the arc, just as G-forces pressed into his chest and his airspeed bled off, he yanked the stick forward and slammed the throttle. The Wildcat dropped like a stone, rolling inverted into a sudden dive.

Teddy leveled off at high speed, the engine howling, and glanced back to see the enemy struggling to regain visual. He yanked into a sharp horizontal turn, trying to reverse their positions. The Zero was slower to respond, caught mid-adjustment.

For a heartbeat, Teddy had the advantage.

He nosed up just slightly, the gunsight tracking the enemy's midsection. He squeezed the trigger.

The cockpit shuddered with recoil. Tracers reached out—bright, deadly fingers. A line of rounds stitched across the Zero's wing. Sparks flew. A thin trail of smoke began curling behind it.

But the Zero's pilot was skilled. It broke left, tightening its turn beyond what the Wildcat could match. Teddy throttled back, letting it pull ahead, then banked right for a high-side pass. The Zero swung back, aggressive, forcing a head-on confrontation. At 500 yards, they both fired—tracers crisscrossing in a deadly lattice. A jolt rocked the Wildcat; something struck his wing, but the aircraft's rugged construction held. He flashed past the Zero, so close he could see the pilot's focused expression.

Now it was a spiraling stalemate, both of them turning hard, neither gaining the upper hand. His fuel gauge dipped lower—he couldn't dogfight forever. The Zero had endurance, and time was on its side.

Teddy had to end it.

He feigned a sloppy, widening turn, inviting the Zero to close in. It took the bait, dropping into a shallow dive to cut him off. At the last second, he snapped into a barrel roll and reversed direction.

And suddenly—it was there. Centered. Perfect. He squeezed the trigger.

The Wildcat shook from the recoil. Rounds tore into the Zero's engine and cockpit. A cloud of smoke erupted, and the plane dipped its nose into a fatal spiral, plummeting toward the sea.

He'd leveled out, watching it fall until it vanished beneath the waves. Then he scanned the sky, every muscle still taut, hands trembling on the stick. The fuel gauge was near empty. But the Wildcat would take him home. It always had.

Lying in the dark now, Teddy exhaled, the remembered roar of the engine fading. The bunk creaked beneath him. Around him, the hum of the ship. Above him, steel. Inside him, silence.

And still, somewhere just behind his eyes, the dogfight replayed itself again.

PAN AMERICAN
PAA

By mid-1942, following the strategic victory at Midway, the United States Navy and Marine Corps shifted from a defensive posture to an aggressive, forward-leaning strategy in the Pacific. This next phase of the war was known as "island hopping."

The objective was to seize key islands across the central and western Pacific, gradually establishing a network of operational bases from which the United States could launch and control air and maritime operations. Each captured island served as a springboard for the next, providing runways for aircraft, anchorages for fleets, and a buffer against Japanese counterattacks.

This strategy bypassed heavily fortified enemy strongholds when possible, instead targeting less-defended but strategically located islands. With each successful "hop," the Allied forces crept closer to the Japanese homeland, tightening the noose and paving the way for eventual victory.

REUNITED IN PARADISE

Upon arriving at Pearl Harbor, Teddy could hardly wait to get a message off to Caroline. With the Enterprise entering a six-week stretch of refitting, repairs, and full restoration to operational readiness, he saw a rare window of calm in the chaos. If he could get her out to Hawaii—if only for a little while—they might finally share the Honolulu moments he'd long dreamed of. The ones he'd envisioned as he'd walked those beaches alone before war erupted.

He knew it wouldn't be easy. Commercial flights were nearly non-existent for civilians, and passage aboard naval ships was typically reserved for essential military personnel or high-priority logistical needs. Still, he held out hope. With six weeks of relative downtime, even two weeks together would feel like a lifetime.

The cable he sent was carefully worded and sent through official Navy channels to her parents in Atlanta. From there, they would know how to reach her—he hoped. It read simply:

"Enterprise in drydock Pearl Harbor. Six weeks here. Any chance you can join me? Love, Teddy."

But Caroline wasn't in Atlanta. She was several thousand miles west, having just delivered a gleaming, brand-new P-38 Lightning to an Army Air Forces base outside San Francisco. She was now officially a part of the Women's Auxiliary Ferrying Squadron, or WAFS—a pioneering group of civilian women pilots who ferried military aircraft from manufacturing plants to airfields across the country. Her schedule had become a whirlwind of cross-country hops, aircraft briefings, mechanical checklists, and nonstop radio chatter.

When she returned to her temporary quarters at Hamilton Field late that evening—dusty from the flight and buzzing from the hum of the Lockheed's twin Allison engines—she found a telegram waiting for her. It had been redirected by her parents.

Caroline read Teddy's words slowly, three times. Her heart soared.

She didn't hesitate. With her WAFS credentials and the support of her commanding officer, she arranged passage aboard a Boeing 314 Clipper scheduled to depart San Francisco for Pearl Harbor in five days. The Clipper flights were reserved for senior military personnel and ferry officers with priority assignments. Luckily, one seat had become available due to a last-minute reassignment.

Her cable back to Teddy was brief but exact:

"Arriving Honolulu on Clipper, five days from now. Can't wait. I have a surprise for you. – Caroline"

When Teddy read it, he broke into a wide grin, holding the message to his chest. Five days. He could wait five days. Maybe.

Each day crawled. He threw himself into training, pushing himself and his squadron through advanced combat drills. They practiced simulated dogfights, tactical formations, carrier takeoffs and landings, and evasive maneuvers. Lessons from the Coral Sea and Midway were being passed from squadron to squadron —hard-won experience inked in blood and fuel.

And there was more.

His commanding officer pulled him aside during a debrief and handed him a folded piece of paper. Teddy opened it slowly. It was a recommendation for the Distinguished Flying Cross, recognizing his actions during the last major sortie, where he had shot down multiple enemy aircraft while protecting the fleet.

He didn't know what to say. He folded the paper again, tucked it into his breast pocket, and quietly returned to the mess tent.

There was no time to reflect—not yet. He was now officially promoted to lieutenant, and a gold bar ceremony was scheduled for the following week. With the promotion came new responsibility: he was to command a full twelve-plane Wildcat squadron. No longer just a pilot, he was now a leader, and the lives of eleven others would depend on his judgment and skill.

Rumors swirled about the arrival of the Grumman F6F Hellcat—a faster, more powerful fighter built to match the Japanese Zero. But official word was that the Enterprise would not yet receive them. For now, they would continue flying the rugged, dependable Wildcats.

The fifth day arrived, warm and breezy. By late afternoon, the golden light of early evening bathed the harbor in honeyed tones as Teddy made his way to the shoreline base terminal.

Passengers began disembarking—naval officers, transport crew, and ferry pilots in khaki uniforms. Teddy scanned each face eagerly. Then he saw her.

She was near the rear of the group, a duffel slung over her shoulder, her cap pulled down just slightly. She looked tired. And aglow.

He almost didn't recognize her—she wore a full WAFS uniform, her pilot wings glinting in the sunlight.

"Caroline?" he called out, hesitant.

She turned, eyes lighting up.

"Surprise," she said, dropping her bag as he rushed to her. "I'm flying too."

Teddy wrapped her in a tight embrace, lifting her off the ground.

"You're full of surprises," he whispered against her hair.

They laughed, and when they finally pulled apart, he grabbed her bag and offered his arm.

As they walked toward a waiting taxi, she explained everything.

"I've been flying for the WAFS since January. They fast-tracked me through training in Houston. At first, I flew AT-6s and PT-19 trainers—nothing too fancy—but last month I ferried my first pursuit plane, a P-40 Warhawk. That was wild. Heavy nose, quick on the stick. And last week? My baby. A P-38 Lightning."

Teddy looked at her, eyes wide. "Seriously? The twin-boom interceptor?"

She nodded proudly. "Twin Allison engines, counter-rotating props. Climbs like a hawk, cruises at over 300 knots, and can hit 400 in a dive. I didn't want to give her up."

"Damn," he said, smiling. "That's no milk run. What was it like?"

"Smooth," she said. "Responsive. You feel like you're riding a stallion that just happens to have machine guns in its nose. The cockpit visibility is amazing—panoramic. But she's a diva. You have to watch your torque and engine temps constantly. One wrong move and she'll spin out on you."

They climbed into the taxi, and as it pulled away, Caroline asked, "So what about you? What have you been doing since Pearl?"

Teddy hesitated, watching the palm trees whip by.

"That," he said, squeezing her hand gently, "is a conversation for later."

They arrived at the Moana Hotel on Waikiki Beach, one of the few civilian accommodations still accepting military guests on R&R. Teddy had managed to secure a modest room with a view of the ocean. As they stepped out of the taxi, the scent of sea salt and plumeria filled the air. Waves rolled gently onto the shore as if welcoming them both.

Upstairs, the bellhop opened the shutters to reveal a picture-perfect scene: the sun was beginning to dip low over the Pacific, casting the surf in gold.

Teddy set her bag down and pulled her close again.

"I thought of this moment a thousand times," he said. "Now it's real."

They stood quietly for a moment, listening to the distant murmur of waves.

Then Caroline turned, her fingers brushing the gold lieutenant bar on his collar.

"I'm proud of you," she said.

He smiled. "They think I deserve a medal."

"You do."

They sat side-by-side on the lanai, their hands intertwined, watching the sky fade from blue to amber.

And for the first time in months, neither of them had anywhere else they needed to be.

While there was a brief lull in action across the Pacific, the war raged fiercely elsewhere—most critically in the Atlantic. The Allies were facing staggering losses in the Battle of the Atlantic, as German U-boats ravaged merchant convoys supplying Britain and the Soviet Union. These submarines operated in coordinated wolf packs, exploiting a deadly gap in air coverage over the mid-Atlantic.

This "air gap" was the most dangerous zone in the ocean—beyond the range of Allied land-based aircraft and rich hunting grounds for German subs. In response, the U.S. Navy and Royal Navy began producing and deploying escort destroyers—smaller, fast-moving ships equipped with sonar and depth charges—to protect convoys. These helped, but without full aerial surveillance, losses remained unsustainably high.

The turning point came with the arrival of long-range bombers like the B-24 Liberator, adapted for maritime patrol. Once these aircraft could spot U-boats from the air, the tide began to turn. But at this stage of the war, the Allies were still losing the battle—and every convoy that survived was a hard-earned victory.

RETURN TO THE FLAME

The water steamed as it poured over their bodies, curling around their skin like the trailing breath of a sigh. Teddy stood behind Caroline, hands gliding over her shoulders, slick with soap and warmth. She leaned into him, her hair wet against his chest, her breath shallow. He cupped her hips gently, the feel of her skin smooth and alive beneath his fingers. She turned to face him, water cascading between them, and smiled—a smile that knew every mile they'd endured to be here, every ache of longing that now found release.

Their mouths met, tender and hungry, and the kiss deepened as his hand slid up the curve of her back. She lathered her palms, reaching around to trace the lather over his chest, his arms, down. He sucked in his breath, not from surprise but from the sheer intensity of her touch. He returned the favor, taking the soap in hand and drawing it across her breasts, down the soft line of her belly. Their movements were unhurried but pulsing with urgency. Steam cloaked the shower stall as they pressed close, lips exploring, hands rediscovering the contours of love.

Water beaded on her eyelashes as she whispered, "Come to bed."

They emerged from the steam hand in hand, Teddy with a towel slung around his hips, Caroline wrapped in one, her skin flushed and dewy from the heat. He kissed her temple, then the line of her jaw, savoring the taste of her skin and the way she leaned into him, trusting and serene.

She backed toward the bed, eyes locked with his, her mouth curved in a sultry, knowing smile. He let his towel fall without hesitation. She followed, letting the towel slip off her shoulders and flutter to the floor like the last barrier giving way to desire.

Moonlight spilled through the slats of the blinds, striping the bed in silver. Teddy stood still for a moment, drinking her in—shoulders bare, nipples peaked from the cool air, the curve of her waist drawing his gaze downward like a magnetic pull.

He moved toward her slowly, predator and worshipper all at once, climbing onto the bed and trailing kisses from her mouth down the slope of her neck. She arched her back, her hands already exploring the muscles in his arms and the firm line of his spine.

He took his time, deliberately kissing the hollow of her throat, then her sternum, then lower, brushing his lips over the soft swells of her breasts. Caroline trembled beneath him as his tongue traced delicate circles around her nipple before he took it into his mouth. She let out a gasp and twisted a fist into the sheets.

"Teddy..." she whispered, and he responded by giving the same attention to the other breast, one hand cradling her ribs while the other slowly slid down the centerline of her body, fingers spreading warmth across her stomach.

He kissed down her belly with reverence, letting his lips trail just beneath her navel, pausing to breathe her in. She writhed slightly, her thighs parting in anticipation. He ran his hands down the insides of her legs, fingertips grazing her skin like a spark, coaxing moans from her with every inch he covered.

Caroline reached down, her fingers running through his hair, guiding him closer. Teddy's mouth hovered over her hip as his hands explored between her thighs—gentle at first, then more insistent, drawing pleasure from her with the precision of a man who knew her well and wanted to know her better still.

He moved back up her body, kissing her stomach

again, then her ribs, then her mouth—hungry now, the slow burn of their foreplay having turned to an urgent fire. She pulled him on top of her, wrapping her legs around his waist.

"I want you," she murmured, voice rough and wanting.

Teddy entered her slowly, savoring the way she gasped and clutched at his back. They stayed still, pressed together in perfect stillness, eyes locked. Then they began to move, their rhythm building gradually, fueled by weeks of longing and the memory of skin and heat and love.

She clung to him as he drove deeper, her breath catching with each stroke. He whispered her name against her lips, her throat, her ear, and she moaned in response, her nails dragging lightly down his back. He cupped her breast again, thumb brushing her nipple as she arched and cried out, her body tense with nearing climax.

"Come with me," he whispered, voice hoarse.

Their pace quickened, hips meeting with unrelenting need until Caroline cried out his name, her body trembling beneath his. He followed, groaning against her shoulder as his own climax claimed him, every muscle taut and straining before he finally collapsed beside her.

They lay tangled in the sheets, breathless, flushed, slick with sweat and love and a sense of something sacred. Teddy pulled her close, one arm draped over her waist, his other hand brushing her hair back from her face.

Caroline nestled into him with a contented sigh, her fingers tracing lazy circles on his chest.

"I never forgot," she whispered.

"Me neither," he said, pressing a kiss to the top of her head.

The next morning, they were awoken by a knock at the door. Startled, Teddy grabbed for a t-shirt. Another knock came as he approached and opened the door to a young sailor.

"Good morning, Lieutenant. You're being called back to the base," the sailor said, handing him an envelope.

"Thank you, sailor."

Teddy closed the door and opened the envelope, expecting some sort of urgent mission or training recall. Instead, he found instructions to report at noon in full dress whites for a press conference. The Navy was announcing his receipt of the Distinguished Flying Cross.

Apparently, the press corps wanted to meet one of the first aces of the Pacific War, and with five-and-a-half confirmed kills, Teddy fit the bill.

He prepared himself quietly and kissed Caroline goodbye. They had agreed it was best not to appear as a couple in public—at least not yet.

At the press conference, Teddy answered every question with humility, deflecting credit to his squadron, his wingmen, and plain luck. The photographers snapped his image as he stood straight and solemn in his whites.

Returning to the hotel that afternoon, he stepped inside and found Caroline waiting.

"How'd it go?" she asked.

"Meeting the press is harder than a dogfight," he replied.

They laughed as the door closed behind them.

The Guadalcanal campaign, which began in August of 1942, marked the first major Allied offensive against Japanese forces in the Pacific. While the focus was on securing a small airstrip—later named Henderson Field—the operation quickly spiraled into a prolonged and brutal struggle on land, in the air, and especially at sea.

American forces, particularly the Navy, paid a staggering price to hold the island. In a series of chaotic and often confused night engagements known collectively as the Naval Battles of Guadalcanal, the United States lost multiple cruisers, including the USS Quincy, USS Vincennes, and USS Astoria, as well as destroyers and hundreds of sailors. For many, the dark waters around Savo Island became synonymous with death.

Yet out of this costly and painful campaign came vital lessons. The Navy was forced to adapt to night fighting, improve coordination between surface ships and aircraft, and develop better logistical support for forward operations. Perhaps most importantly, Guadalcanal proved that Japan could be stopped—and that American resolve, even when bloodied, would not break.

THE WEAVE

Days in Honolulu passed quickly for Teddy and Caroline. Caroline basked in the warm sun of Waikiki Beach during the day while Teddy worked with his squadron on tactics. His days were full of flying, classroom sessions, and learning the demanding role of a squadron leader. That meant not only mastering the skies but also tackling a mountain of administrative responsibilities—something he didn't enjoy, but he managed, nonetheless.

Their evenings were spent in long moonlit strolls, private dinners, and intimate moments of connection and love. The beauty of Oahu, the warm trade winds, and the temporary reprieve from war wrapped their days in an almost dreamlike haze. But like all dreams, it had to end. Not because Teddy was being called out to sea, but because Caroline's leave was up—she had to return to her duties with the Women's Auxiliary Ferrying Squadron.

After only ten days together, Teddy escorted Caroline to the wharf where the Pan Am Clipper awaited for her flight back to the mainland. She was back in uniform now, looking smart and composed. Teddy was in his flight suit, planning to report back to base the moment she departed. They hugged and kissed, murmuring soft promises to be careful and to write often. They laughed when they both said it at the same time—neither needed to be reminded.

Then Teddy pulled her close and whispered, "Again, a kiss goodbye."

The kiss lingered, full of memory and yearning. Caroline slowly pulled back, gave him one last glance, picked up her bag, and ascended the gangplank. Teddy stood alone, watching the clipper taxi and then lift off, its sleek wings glinting in the sun. He waved even though he couldn't see her through the windows.

Teddy returned to base where the day's schedule listed an important training tactic: the Thach Weave.

Gathering his pilots, Teddy stood before a chalkboard and began to explain. The Thach Weave was a revolutionary defensive flying maneuver developed by Lieutenant Commander John Thach during the early days of the Pacific War. In essence, it allowed two American fighters to defend one another against a more agile enemy—particularly the Japanese Zero.

Teddy illustrated two planes flying in a parallel course, separated by some distance. When attacked by a more maneuverable enemy fighter, each plane would begin turning toward the other in a weaving pattern. If the enemy followed one of them, that attacker would unknowingly be drawn into the line of fire of the second plane. The crisscrossing flight paths meant no single aircraft was ever isolated, and the attacker risked becoming the hunted.

"The key is communication and spacing," Teddy explained. "We stay close enough to support, far enough not to collide. If you're being tailed, don't panic—just turn in toward your wingman and trust the weave. We protect each other."

His squadron practiced the maneuver in the air, pairing up and flying deliberate, slow weaves before increasing their speed and fluidity. The improvement was immediate. Confidence grew. Pilots felt safer, empowered by the tactic. It became a cornerstone of their defensive training.

Shortly after the exercise, Teddy was summoned to a strategic meeting with the base commander and fellow squadron leaders. Around the long table sat Navy pilots, operational planners, and Marine Corps liaisons. Maps were spread out but destinations remained classified.

Still, the nature of the meeting made clear that operations were accelerating.

Their briefing outlined the evolving strategy in the Pacific: successive strikes against key Japanese-held islands, designed to shrink the enemy's reach and prepare for eventual moves toward the Japanese homeland. Though the term "island hopping" wasn't officially uttered, the implication was clear.

The mission profile was shifting. While air-to-air combat would always remain a priority, carrier-based fighters were now tasked with more air-to-ground operations—close air support for Marines engaged on beaches and jungles below.

Teddy leaned in as plans were reviewed. There were discussions about strafing runs, dive-bombing techniques, and ordnance adjustments. Bomb loads would need tweaking. Armor-piercing shells might be replaced with fragmentation bombs or incendiaries, depending on the target. He took notes and conferred with his fellow squadron leaders, trying to absorb every tactical nuance.

Though he missed Caroline already, the intensity of the coming mission consumed him. There was no time to dwell. As the Enterprise prepared to set sail once again, Teddy focused his mind on leading his men into a new phase of the war—one that demanded precision, courage, and teamwork from the skies above.

Years before the war began, Japanese naval engineers made a critical choice: they prioritized speed and striking power over survivability. This philosophy deeply influenced the design of their warships, especially their destroyers—fast, agile, and heavily armed with torpedoes, but with minimal armor. These ships became known among American sailors as "tin cans," a grim reference to their inability to withstand even light enemy fire.

While Japanese destroyers were admired for their maneuverability and offensive reach, they were tragically under protected for modern naval warfare. In battles like Leyte Gulf, they charged into overwhelming odds with little more than courage and thin steel to shield them. One solid hit often meant disaster—engines crippled, fires spreading uncontrollably, or the entire ship lost within minutes.

Though their aircraft carriers suffered similar vulnerabilities, with flight decks lacking armor and damage control systems inferior to those of the Americans, it was the destroyers that most embodied Japan's design flaw. Built to attack but not to endure, they became both a testament to bold engineering and a costly strategic miscalculation.

THE DESTROYER

The USS Enterprise had moved into striking range of Guadalcanal, just days before the planned invasion. The Rough Riders—Teddy's squadron of Navy aviators—waited with a restless energy. For the first time in American history, a large-scale amphibious assault would be launched by sea with full Marine support, and no one knew quite what to expect. The risks were enormous. The environment, uncertain. The outcome, unknowable.

In preparation, the Enterprise and its escorts organized a broad perimeter, assigning key responsibilities to its squadrons. Teddy's unit was tasked with aerial patrols to detect and eliminate threats before they could reach the fleet. Three groups of four Wildcats fanned out in a wide triangle around Guadalcanal, covering blind spots and watching for incoming enemy forces. Teddy led the northernmost flight, patrolling between Savo Island and Guadalcanal's jagged northern shore.

After reaching the outer limit of their patrol range without sighting enemy aircraft, Teddy gave the signal to begin a slow return to the carrier. But instead of flying in their standard diamond formation, he gave orders to spread the flight into a lateral line—four Wildcats flying wingtip to wingtip with about 200 yards of separation. The formation gave them a wider visual range, perfect for scouting.

Then came the call. Teddy's wingman crackled through the radio: "Contact—nine o'clock, low on the horizon. Looks like a destroyer."

Teddy squinted and saw the vessel. With the sun glinting off the ocean, its silhouette confirmed what his cockpit recognition manual would soon verify: a Japanese Kagerō-class destroyer—fast, heavily armed, and likely serving as a screen for enemy naval movement, or worse, as early protection for a major force slipping into the area.

Teddy ordered an immediate reformation of the

flight into combat spacing. "We'll make one run—bow to stern," he said. "Take out the deck crew and disable as much of their AA as we can. Then regroup."

As the Wildcats began their descent, the destroyer's lookouts spotted them. Alarms rang out on the ship's deck. Crewmen sprinted to their stations, rotating 25mm anti-aircraft cannons and preparing dual-purpose 5-inch guns. The destroyer began evasive maneuvering, zigzagging as best it could, but it was too late—the first of the Rough Riders was already diving.

Teddy led the charge. He came in high and fast, then dropped into a shallow dive along the axis of the destroyer's deck. As he pressed the trigger, his six .50-caliber Brownings roared to life, sending hundreds of rounds downrange per second. His tracers stitched the deck from bow to stern. A gun crew manning a forward 25mm emplacement was caught mid-turn and thrown backwards in a burst of flame and shrapnel. Crates of ammunition near midship exploded as another Wildcat raked the centerline.

The air around Teddy turned white-hot with tracer fire. Shells burst beneath his wings, punching holes in the fuselage and spattering his canopy with smoke. One round clipped the edge of his right aileron, causing a momentary roll before he corrected. The second Wildcat passed above him, firing wide and missing the bridge but hitting the stern, sending crewmen diving for cover. The third and fourth fighters strafed with precision—one taking out the port-side gun mount, the other igniting fuel drums near the funnel, creating a geyser of black smoke.

With deck chaos achieved, Teddy reassembled his flight. "Minor damage, but we're flying," his wingman radioed. "I've got a nicked elevator, but nothing serious."

Teddy could see the destroyer was far from crippled. Its main guns were still intact, and it was accelerating hard to port. He made a quick decision. "Second pass. We go low—waterline. Aim for the engine room."

The Wildcats banked and came around in a wide arc. This time, they flew in staggered intervals just above sea level. The destroyer now fully alerted, turned its dual-purpose guns toward the low-flying aircraft. The second wave met with ferocious resistance. Teddy's cockpit filled with the thump of concussions. Splinters from near-misses cracked the outer canopy of one of the wingmen, and smoke curled from the engine cowling of another.

Still, they pressed on. Teddy aimed low and squeezed. His .50-cal rounds peppered the steel hull right at the waterline. Sparks flew, and a panel of hull plating buckled under the assault. The third Wildcat hit just behind the funnel, and a large secondary explosion indicated a possible fuel tank rupture. The destroyer's speed dropped noticeably, and its course became erratic. Water foamed as it struggled to steer.

Teddy's flight regrouped once more. Ammunition was nearly exhausted. He issued the final run order: "One more sweep—then we pull back."

The last strafing run was brutal. With only seconds of ammunition left, each pilot emptied their belts in controlled, punishing bursts. One Wildcat's rounds tore through the remaining starboard AA crew just as they attempted to fire. Another hit the base of the destroyer's bridge, sending an arc of flame through the communications mast. Teddy's own pass cut through the midsection again, and this time, he saw water gushing through a jagged hole just above the waterline.

With their ammunition gone, the Rough Riders pulled up and began wide circles overhead. The destroyer was dead in the water. Smoke poured from three sections of the ship, and the bow was beginning to rise—slowly but unmistakably. The vessel was listing hard to port. Within minutes, the stern dipped below the surface. Flames danced on the oily water as the destroyer's silhouette faded, inch by inch, beneath the Pacific.

"Confirmed sinking," Teddy radioed. "She's going down."

The squadron turned westward and began the flight back to the Enterprise, hearts pounding and adrenaline fading. The radio cracked with laughter, cheers, and disbelief. "A destroyer," one pilot shouted. "We actually sank one!"

Upon arrival, the flight deck was electric. Word had traveled fast. The deck crew waved them in with uncharacteristic exuberance, and sailors clapped and shouted from the catwalks. As each Wildcat taxied in, sailors crowded around, slapping wings and thumping fuselages.

Teddy climbed out of his cockpit and was nearly pulled off his ladder by a dozen hands. "What did she look like going down?" "Was it really a Kagerō?" "You boys did it!"

The ship's air boss was waiting. "The Captain's on his way," he said, grinning.

Within minutes, the commanding officer of the Enterprise arrived on the hangar deck—rare for someone of his rank. He walked straight to Teddy, shook his hand, and said, "Well done, Lieutenant. That's a hell of a first."

In the ready room, the celebration continued. A bottle of contraband whiskey appeared, passed from hand to hand. Mechanics, cooks, radio men—all came by to shake hands and slap backs. Teddy's flight engineer leaned in and said, "We don't have a stencil for a destroyer, sir. But we'll make one."

And they did. By morning, a crisp silhouette of a Japanese destroyer had been stenciled just below Teddy's cockpit canopy, flanked by the five and a half flags already there. Unlike the flags, which marked individual aerial kills, this one marked something shared—a victory achieved by teamwork, daring, and a willingness to press the attack just a little longer.

Below deck, sailors retold the story again and again— how four Wildcats had gone head-to-head with a Kagerō-class ship and sent her to the bottom. For that night at least, aboard the Enterprise, the Rough Riders were legends.

The Guadalcanal Campaign had tested every sinew of American resolve. Over six months of brutal jungle combat, disease, and relentless naval engagements had cost dearly in blood and steel—but at last, it was over. Henderson Field stood operational, its perimeter now secure under the watchful eyes of American Marines, and the battered remains of the once-formidable Imperial Japanese Navy were withdrawing northward. It was a victory, yes—but one paid for in full by the young men who flew and fought and bled for every inch of jungle dirt.

THE TRIANGLE ISLAND RUN

For Teddy Davidson and the Rough Riders aboard the USS Enterprise, it was a bittersweet milestone. The carrier had maintained her station off Guadalcanal during those final days, offering her fliers a strange new rhythm—no longer just support for the embattled Marines, but active reconnaissance of the Solomon Islands chain for remaining Japanese positions and signs of enemy withdrawal or reinforcement.

The days had become routine: launch at first light, scout, and return by midday if the skies were kind. That morning had begun no differently. Teddy led a twelve-plane formation into the golden haze of dawn, the Wildcats gleaming in the early light, bristling with full loads of .50 caliber ammunition and auxiliary fuel tanks. His wingmen were alert but relaxed. They had grown used to this rhythm—patrolling skies that no longer swarmed with Zeros, circling jungle-covered islands that had once bristled with flak.

They flew a lazy sweep northwest before turning southeast again. They were still within distance of the Enterprise, still within radio contact. The tanks were more than half full. Spirits were high.

That's when Ensign Wirth crackled in over the comms. "Lead, this might be nothing, but check out that triangle ahead—looks like a volcano blew its top once upon a time."

Teddy scanned the horizon. There it was—an oddly shaped triangle of land about seven miles off their return course. A jagged ridge marked the western slope, the remnants of volcanic rock still bleeding black scars through the jungle. The eastern side dropped into a steep cliff, leveling into a green shelf above a bright, crescent-shaped bay—steep, barren, and silent.

"Alright," Teddy called. "We'll take a look. Keep it tight. No heroics."

As they banked toward the island, Teddy spotted something unnatural through the trees—a glint of metal, parallel lines carved unnaturally through the underbrush. An airstrip. Hidden. Narrow. Primitive—but unmistakably active. The jungle around it had been cleared just enough to conceal its form from distance. Camo netting and palm fronds had been laid across munitions' shacks and revetments.

And parked along the crude runway: enemy fighters. At least a dozen, tightly packed. Zeros, most of them, their wings tucked like folded blades. A few appeared fueled and ready. All of them were vulnerable.

"Holy hell," murmured Lieutenant King. "They've got a full nest down there."

Teddy didn't hesitate. "Form up. Line attack. I want everyone to take one pass. Focus on the aircraft. Let's light them up."

Twelve Wildcats peeled into a shallow dive in perfect order, fanning out into attack formation. Teddy led the run, dropping first with throttle open and tracers hot. His .50 caliber guns stitched a line of fire through a pair of parked fighters—one disintegrated instantly, while the other caught a wingtip and burst into flame.

The rest followed in staggered succession. Harding tore through fuel drums; the explosion knocked a maintenance shed off its supports. Rios strafed a Zero with open cowling, slicing its exposed engine block. Carmichael clipped a hangar roof but stayed in the fight, laying suppressing fire across camouflaged crates. One exploded—ammunition—sending a ring of fire through the revetments like a fuse.

Fires bloomed. Fuel tanks ruptured. Smoke towered upward. The jungle fringe caught embers; palm trunks crackled. Trees bent outward, fronds disintegrating under the blowtorch wind of the firestorm. Japanese troops scattered into the jungle, some firing rifles skyward in panic.

The squadron's formation stayed lethal. They came down the strip like clockwork. Wildcat after Wildcat dove low and let loose. The roar of .50 caliber fire echoed off cliffs. It wasn't just a hit—it was annihilation.

But with fire came response. Anti-aircraft fire opened from cleverly camouflaged guns. Sandbagged nests swung across the runway's edge. Flak burst in white blossoms. Teddy's fliers radioed in light damage—until Wirth's voice cut in:

"Lead—I'm hit. Engine's on fire. She's—she's not holding!"

Teddy jerked his head around. Wirth's Wildcat belched black smoke, flames licking the cowling. He nosed toward the western shoreline and bailed out. The chute opened fast. He splashed down 300 yards offshore, well within range of the Japanese jungle.

Then came the gunfire—muzzle flashes from the palms. Rounds peppered the water.

"Form a Lufbery Circle. Keep that beach suppressed. Nobody touches our boy."

They broke into a Lufbery Circle—nose to tail, a rotating defensive ring. Named after Raoul Lufbery, a World War I ace, it allowed each pilot to cover the one ahead. Today, it served a more aggressive role: continuous strafing. Teddy dove first, firing into the treeline. Palm trunks splintered. Gun pits cracked open. Each pilot followed. The rhythm was ruthless, efficient. The edge of the jungle became a mess of shredded wood and fire.

Teddy broke radio silence. "Enterprise, this is Rough Leader. Found enemy strip. Took it out. One man down off west shore. Requesting SAR—search and rescue. Need cover and relief ASAP. We're low on fuel."

"Copy, Rough Leader. SAR inbound. Second wave scrambled."

Search and Rescue—SAR—was the protocol. A floatplane or scout aircraft would recover downed pilots. In this case, an SOC Seagull biplane launched from a cruiser. Lightly armed, they depended on fighter cover.

Minutes later, the Seagull skimmed over the ocean, angling toward Wirth.

Then the jungle erupted.

A hidden AA gun opened up. A burst tore through the Seagull's fuselage. It cartwheeled into the ocean, a fireball on impact.

"No!" someone yelled.

"Finish your belts!" Teddy ordered. "Suppress that beach."

The Rough Riders dove once more. Some had only seconds of ammo left. The shoreline dissolved in smoke and flame. Wirth floated alone, bobbing in his Mae West.

"RTB," Teddy said. "Save fuel. We'll be back."

They turned home. Two Wildcats trailed smoke. Hydraulics were out on one. They'd make it.

The second wave was already inbound—twelve fresh Wildcats. They resumed the Lufbery Circle.

Two were hit. One spiraled into the jungle. The other lost a wing—its pilot bailed, drifting eastward on the wind toward the volcanic cliffs.

That eastern slope was steep, silent, unoccupied. The downed pilots landed there. Safe—for now.

But Ensign Wirth remained adrift, watching the sky and the jungle beyond it, as the sun fell behind the ridge.

While vast battles raged across the globe, a very different kind of struggle was underway within the United States—a secret race to unlock the most destructive force ever harnessed by mankind. Launched in the fall of 1942, the Manhattan Project aimed to use nuclear science to build a weapon so powerful it might end the war outright, potentially eliminating the need for a costly invasion of Japan—or even Germany. But uncertainties loomed. No one knew if such a weapon could be built in time, whether it could be deployed safely, or if its existence could remain hidden. For those fighting and dying in the Pacific, with no knowledge of this secret weapon, the war dragged on—demanding immense courage, sacrifice, and endurance.

WORTH SAVING

Teddy's boots hadn't been on the flight deck more than five minutes before the hangar bays swallowed up the wounded aircraft. Of the eleven Wildcats that returned from the Triangle Island assault, six were too damaged to rearm quickly and were sent down to the hangar deck for repairs. But naval efficiency and preparation were in full swing. Five replacement aircraft were already being hoisted up from below, fueled and armed, their canopies open, engines pre-warmed.

That left ten planes to rejoin the fight—Teddy's Rough Riders, regrouped and refitted.

Teddy took a hard swig of lukewarm coffee and downed half a sandwich while walking. His flight suit still smelled of cordite and engine oil. Around him, ground crews worked like a pit crew at Indianapolis, their movements practiced, synchronized, urgent. The word had already spread across the deck: Ensign Wirth was still out there.

He made his way to Flight Ops, where the situation was being assessed in quiet, tense tones. The Admiral and his staff weren't working from maps—because there were none. The island had no name, no chart, no contour lines. Instead, a rough sketch covered the clear plastic plotting board above the chart table. Someone had drawn its triangular shape with a grease pencil directly on the plexiglass overlay, using Teddy's verbal description and radio reports from the first and second flights.

Small circles marked the airstrip, the fuel dump, the jungle edge. A jagged line represented the volcanic cliffs on the eastern side, and a star marked where Wirth had gone down. It was crude, but it was all they had.

Teddy pointed to the western shoreline. "We were seeing muzzle flashes from here, in this brush line. Probably emplacements just behind the palms. But we never saw the full layout—too much foliage."

The Admiral tapped the grease pencil against the circle labeled "AA gun (suspected)" and nodded. "Then this is where the SAR needs cover."

"We've committed thirty-five planes," one officer reported. "Stacked in three concentric Lufbery Circles, offset by altitude."

Teddy raised a brow. "That's the biggest circle I've ever heard of."

The Admiral nodded. "We're building an aerial shield—layered fire. If anyone on that island so much as blinks in Wirth's direction, they'll be shot before they finish the motion."

They knew the problem wasn't just fire suppression. It was retrieval.

The first SAR had been a failure. The SOC Seagull had gone down in flames. Two aviators dead. And that had shaken the brass. Getting another bird into that kill zone without cover was suicide.

Meanwhile, on the far side of the island—the eastern volcanic cliffs—a Navy destroyer had maneuvered into the deep water and launched a small crew ashore. Those sailors, rappelling into the black rock and gnarled scrub, had recovered the two downed pilots from the second wave and brought them safely aboard. A small victory.

But the western shore—the beach where Wirth floated—remained hostile, shallow, and largely unmapped. Too dangerous for a ship to approach.

"We'll need to try another seaplane," one of the officers said. "There's no way around it."

Teddy spoke up. "Then give it cover. What if we deployed a smokescreen over the beach? Enough to blind the enemy for sixty seconds?"

The Admiral glanced up. "With what?"

"TBD Avengers," Teddy answered. "Equip them with smoke canisters in place of torpedoes. Let them fly low and light it up. We time it with the Lufbery Circle and use the Wildcats to rake the tree line."

The Admiral gave a slow nod. "Why use one when you can use four? Make it a wall of smoke."

Orders were dispatched immediately. Below deck, four Avengers were pulled from torpedo rotation and outfitted with heavy smoke dispensers. The torpedo bays were loaded with racks of canisters, and their belly doors were modified to deploy on a signal. It was a bold plan—risky at low altitude, but the best chance they had.

By the time Teddy reached his Wildcat, the deck crew had waved the first eleven planes into position. He climbed into the cockpit, strapped in, and began his pre-check. One by one, the Rough Riders taxied into line. The four Avengers followed, their broader silhouettes rising over the deck like dark vultures.

From a nearby cruiser, a second SOC Seagull—this one launched on floats—took to the sky and held position out of range, awaiting Teddy's signal to begin its approach.

Once airborne, the Rough Riders rejoined the massive Lufbery Circle. Now stacked in layered altitudes, the formation of thirty-five planes spun like a revolving thunderhead over the shoreline. It was one of the largest Lufbery Circles ever assembled in the Pacific. Originating in the skies of World War I, the tactic had evolved from a desperate defense to a deadly rotating assault line. Today, it offered a seamless barrage—while one set of fighters climbed to rejoin the loop, others dove to attack. At any given moment, a Wildcat's guns were spitting fire at the beach.

Teddy's squadron made several coordinated passes, further suppressing enemy positions. But it wasn't just about destruction—it was about timing. The beach had to be blinded.

At last, the signal came.

"Avengers inbound," Flight Ops relayed. "Smoke run in thirty seconds."

The Avengers peeled away from high altitude and descended rapidly to 40 feet above the ocean surface, spreading out in a horizontal line—four abreast, each separated by just over 100 yards. They moved in unison, flying level and low, hugging the shore. Behind them, the Wildcats ramped up their assault. Two planes at a time flew side by side, sweeping the jungle and treetops with blistering .50-caliber fire. Every exposed gun nest, every suspected hide, every canopy gap was lit up.

The Avengers reached the drop point and triggered their smoke.

Billowing columns of white and gray poured out in thick clouds, rolling back over the beach and creeping into the tree line like fog blown by fire. The wall took only 40 seconds to form—and once it did, visibility was gone. The island's entire western edge disappeared beneath a shroud of man-made weather.

Teddy keyed his mic. "Now. Bring in the bird."

The Seagull, waiting just offshore, banked into its final approach.

Beneath the smoke, the Wildcats kept strafing—blind, but practiced. They tore through the veil with controlled passes, ensuring any remaining enemy fire would stay down.

The Seagull emerged over the water, slipping beneath the fog layer like a ghost. It hit the waves cleanly, bounced once, then coasted on its floats directly to Wirth's position. In the haze, it was nearly invisible to any potential sniper. A rescue swimmer popped the hatch, leaned out, and grabbed the floating aviator.

"Rescue has him," came the report. "They're moving out."

The Seagull didn't return to the *Enterprise*—carriers couldn't recover seaplanes. Instead, it flew directly back to the cruiser from which it had launched. Wirth would later be ferried to the *Enterprise* aboard a transfer launch.

The two downed pilots rescued by the destroyer had also been transferred. That evening, all three were ferried in together, climbing up the side netting with help from crewmen, and soon after, escorted below.

The ready room was already full. Pilots, mechanics, junior officers, even a chaplain stood inside as the three rescued men walked in. Applause exploded. Mugs of coffee were lifted in toast. Someone passed around stale sugar cookies. Someone else played Glenn Miller from a battered phonograph.

The Admiral stepped forward. "Some would say we risked too much for one man," he said. "They'd be wrong."

A hush followed.

"If it were you out there, we'd come for you too," he said. "And if it's ever me, I expect the same."

Wirth raised his mug. "Sir... we'd fly solo down the main street of Tokyo if you asked."

The room shook with cheers and laughter.

Later, as things quieted, Teddy and Wirth found a seat together. "I didn't think I'd make it," Wirth said softly.

"You did," Teddy said. "And they'll do it again. For you. For any of us."

Wirth nodded slowly. "I'll never forget it."

Teddy gave him a faint smile. "That's the point."

Outside, the stars blinked through a rising mist. Inside, brothers in arms celebrated the rescue no one believed could succeed. And for one quiet moment, the war held its breath.

The celebration continued long past sunset. One of the mechanics pulled out a harmonica and played a ragged version of "Anchors Aweigh." Someone else produced a deck of cards and called for a round of poker with cigarette rations as the ante. The chaplain sat quietly at the edge, sipping coffee and watching with a small smile on his face. There were no sermons here— only the quiet affirmation of life.

"Toast!" someone shouted. "To the Avengers! They flew lower than my Aunt Sally's porch swing!"

More laughter. One of the Avengers pilots stood up and gave a mock bow. "And I owe that porch swing an apology!"

Even the Admiral chuckled at that one.

Teddy eventually slipped away from the noise. He walked the darkened passageways until he found the ladder to the flight deck. It was quiet up top—just the steady thrum of the ship's movement and the salty Pacific wind on his face. He walked out onto the deck and leaned against the railing. The ocean stretched endlessly, lit faintly by a rising moon.

Footsteps approached. Wirth joined him.

They stood in silence for a long time.

"I don't think I can go back up tomorrow," Wirth said finally.

"You don't have to," Teddy replied.

"I know. But I probably will."

Teddy nodded. "That's how you'll know you're ready."

Wirth let out a long breath. "You ever get used to the fear?"

"No. You just stop letting it boss you around."

Wirth smiled faintly. "That's not in the flight manual."

"It should be."

They stood together as the carrier steamed on, the stars shifting above them, the wake splitting the dark sea like a promise.

Eventually, a voice called from below. "Davidson, ready room. Briefing starts in five."

Teddy nodded toward the hatch. "Back to it."

"See you in the air," Wirth said.

Teddy looked back once before heading below. "Damn right you will."

Down in the ready room, the lights had dimmed. The Admiral stood at the front again, this time with a new chart—one of a different island, farther north, larger, with heavier defenses.

"This was a rescue," he began. "But the next one's a knockout punch. Get some rest, gentlemen. Tomorrow, we go back to work."

The men murmured, settled in. And the war, relentless and waiting, rolled toward them once more.

Later that night, Wirth lay on his bunk, staring at the

metal ceiling above. The ship swayed gently, its rhythm different from the roll of the ocean he had floated in. He could still feel the salt on his skin.

In the quiet, he remembered how long the hours had felt in the water. The sun was blinding. His Mae West kept him afloat, but his legs had cramped. His throat was parched. And every sound—every ripple—had made him brace for something worse.

He had sung to himself to stay awake. "You Are My Sunshine," over and over. Not because it helped, but because it gave him rhythm. Time. Something to push the silence away.

He hadn't cried. Not then. But now, in the dim red light of the sleeping quarters, a few tears escaped quietly, salt on salt. No one noticed. He wiped them away and rolled over.

On the other side of the ship, the Admiral sat alone in his stateroom. The celebration had faded, and only the occasional boots in the corridor reminded him he wasn't alone.

He looked down at the grease-pencil map still clipped to his clipboard—the rough sketch of the triangle island. So much guessing. So many unknowns.

He had ordered four Avengers into that flak field. If it had failed, he would've lost them. And the SAR plane. And probably another Wildcat or two.

But it hadn't failed. Because they had believed in each other more than they had feared the enemy. That, he thought, was the heart of naval aviation. Trust, executed at 300 knots.

He scribbled one word in the corner of the map before setting it down: "Worth."

Below deck, the ready room was quiet again. Teddy had returned in time for the late-night briefing. Most of the pilots looked half-awake, nursing coffee.

The Admiral stood beside a projected sketch of a new island. It was wider than the triangle island. Denser. A jagged coral fringe surrounded its southern tip. Smoke rose from one quadrant of the recon photo—recent bombing, or a signal.

"Next op's going to hit harder," he said. "This one has a full airstrip, reports of twin-engine bombers, and heavier flak. It's not just an air raid. We're targeting supply infrastructure. We fly at dawn."

Teddy raised a hand. "Any air escort?"

"Negative. You are the escort. And the hammer."

He nodded. Of course.

The Admiral looked around the room. "You all did something remarkable today. But this war isn't won on rescues. It's won on resolve. We strike tomorrow. Dismissed."

As the men stood, gathering charts and gear, Teddy caught Wirth's eye from across the room. Wirth didn't smile. He just nodded.

Teddy returned it.

Outside, the sea rolled forward, black and bottomless. But on the *Enterprise*, the lights burned through the night.

In the Pacific War, island atolls took on growing strategic importance as the Allies pushed westward across the vast ocean. These seemingly insignificant specks—sometimes called "blue diamonds in the sea"—were actually coral reefs that had eroded and filled over time to form tiny landmasses.

Though lacking deepwater ports, these atolls were transformed into emergency landing strips for Allied pilots whose planes had been damaged in combat or had run dangerously low on fuel. Their limited size and remoteness meant they could not sustain full-scale operations, but they became lifelines for survival.

Small garrisons of U.S. Marines were stationed on many of these islets, their primary mission not to wage war, but to rescue downed aviators. Equipment and supplies had to be ferried ashore, and living conditions were often harsh—but the role these makeshift outposts played in saving lives made them indispensable to the Allied war effort.

TRADING IN MY PLANE

Teddy's squadron had settled into a punishing rhythm. By day, they alternated between reconnaissance runs, fleet cover patrols, and ground support for the Marines clawing their way through the jungle and ridges of Guadalcanal. By night, they patched up their planes, debriefed over lukewarm coffee, and tried not to think about how many times they'd barely made it back.

The ground support missions were especially hazardous. While the pilots understood the vital role they played in helping their fellow Americans on the island, few of them relished the duty. Dogfighting—that was what they'd trained for, what they talked about in the ready room, what stirred something primal in them. Strafing runs against entrenched Japanese positions were necessary, but flying low over the treetops meant facing a wall of small-arms fire. The Japanese didn't need radar or spotters—just patience, discipline, and a lucky shot.

Teddy had seen too many of his men return with wings shredded or oil leaking from their cowling. Rarely did a mission end without someone taking damage. To address this, Teddy had spent long hours with the mechanics between sorties, designing modifications to the Wildcats—specifically armor plating beneath the cockpit to protect the pilots from below. It wasn't much, but it might deflect a bullet or two. As he told his squadron, "When you fly over a hundred Japanese rifles, somebody's gonna hit you—even if you're doing two hundred miles an hour."

Whenever possible, the squadron rotated between Henderson Field and the Enterprise. At Henderson, they refueled and rearmed in a dusty, hasty patch of earth carved from the jungle. Repairs were basic—patch it and fly. But aboard the Enterprise, they had proper gear, skilled mechanics, and if they were lucky, a hot meal.

One late afternoon, Teddy was assigned top cover patrol. The squadron would fly a wide arc to the north, where enemy aircraft had been spotted the day before. Teddy, now a seasoned flight leader, had changed tactics. Instead of flying in larger formations, he'd broken the squadron into pairs—more nimble, more flexible, and far better at covering ground. He trusted his men. They knew how to fight, and they didn't need a dozen planes to do it.

At fifteen thousand feet, cruising just beneath high cirrus clouds, Teddy and his wingman leveled out in a long northern sweep. The sun was beginning to dip behind them, casting the Pacific in bands of gold and deep blue. Then—movement.

Two Zekes, flying about three thousand feet below, unaware they'd been spotted.

Teddy tapped his stick twice and tilted his wings—a signal to attack. His wingman acknowledged, and the two Wildcats peeled over in unison, plunging into the dive with the sun at their backs. Altitude was life. Surprise was death—for the enemy.

The attack was over in seconds. Both American planes opened fire in perfect sync, their six .50 caliber guns stitching fire into the silhouettes of the Zekes. The Japanese fighters disintegrated under the barrage, fragments scattering like confetti in the sky. But even in victory came danger. A shard of debris from one of the exploding Zekes smashed into Teddy's cockpit, shattering the forward canopy. Shards of glass and metal whipped past his face, but his goggles saved his eyes. Shaken but in control, he pulled up and leveled off again at fifteen thousand.

Smoke trailed from his fuselage, but the plane held together. He checked over his shoulder—his wingman had damage too, a scorched tail and an oil streak along the port wing. They signaled to each other and turned for home. It had been a clean kill, but it was time to regroup.

They didn't get far.

Below them, at ten thousand feet, four Japanese bombers with two Zeros in escort formation were lumbering along—likely on their way to strike Henderson or the fleet. Teddy's hands gripped the stick tighter. He could have let them go. His plane was already compromised. But something in him refused.

Another signal. Another dive.

Coming in from above and with the sun behind them again, Teddy and his wingman plunged at full throttle. The bombers never had a chance. Teddy lined up and let loose a long burst into the lead aircraft—its left engine burst into flame, and it dropped like a stone. His wingman took the second. The Japanese formation scattered, but not before the Zeros reacted.

They were fast. Within moments, the escorts banked up sharply, each locking onto an American fighter.

The textbook move in a situation like this was the Thach Weave—a maneuver that required two fighters working in tight coordination to cross paths and trap the pursuing enemy. But now, each American had a Zero glued to his tail. There would be no weaving. Just survival.

Teddy juked left, then right, but the Zero stayed on him. He checked his instruments—plenty of altitude. He shoved the stick forward and dove, straight down.

The wind roared. The Wildcat shuddered. He could feel the damage from the earlier explosion—panels rattled, and the left wing trembled. But gravity was his friend now. The Zero followed briefly but couldn't match the dive speed.

By the time Teddy leveled out, the Japanese fighter had broken off, banking away to rejoin the others. But the dive had taken Teddy far off course—north of his patrol sector, away from the Enterprise, and even beyond the edge of the map they'd been assigned.

He pulled up cautiously. The engine whined in protest, and the airframe creaked. Alone now, he scanned the sky—no sign of his wingman, no sign of the bombers, no sign of anything.

The vastness of the Pacific closed in. Just sky, sea, and the sound of his damaged Wildcat, still airborne but far from home.

His fuel gauge was dropping steadily. A return to Enterprise was no longer realistic. Instead, he scanned the horizon for anything—an emergency strip, a clearing, a sliver of sand.

Then he saw it: a tiny atoll, barely more than a strip of white coral and green scrub, surrounded by the turquoise shimmer of the reef. A landing strip had been carved into the narrowest stretch of land, rough but passable.

Teddy brought the Wildcat in low, wheels down, coaxing it toward the patch of dirt and coral. The landing was hard, the wheels bouncing once—twice—before catching. Dust and sand flew up around him as the plane skidded to a halt just yards from the end of the strip.

A handful of Marines ran toward him, rifles slung, shirts unbuttoned against the heat. One of them, a corporal with sunburned cheeks and a pack of Lucky

Strikes tucked into his sleeve, waved Teddy down as he popped the canopy and climbed out.

"Hell of a landing, Lieutenant," the corporal said. "Where'd you come from?"

Teddy pulled off his helmet, sweat-soaked and streaked with grit. "North of Guadalcanal. Got into a scrap with a couple Zekes, then bombers. Lost my wingman. Bird's banged up, but still flies."

The Marines gave low whistles as they circled the Wildcat, noting the scorched tail, the cracked canopy, and the oil streaks.

"Well, you're not the first Wildcat to land here," the corporal said, jerking a thumb toward a nearby patch of palm and scrub.

There, under a tattered camouflage net, sat another Wildcat. Dust-covered, but intact.

"That one showed up a few weeks ago," the Marine continued. "Pilot landed it clean. We saw him climb out, wave once, then bolt into the jungle like the devil was chasing him. Never came back. We searched for three days—nothing. No blood, no gear, no sign of him at all."

Teddy stared at the abandoned plane. "Engine runs?"

"Like a dream. We keep her tuned, just in case. And now it looks like that case just walked in."

One of the younger Marines, wide-eyed and eager, asked, "Did you shoot any bandits?"

Teddy nodded. "Yeah. I got two."

"Well, don't you think we oughta get your gun camera footage before you leave?" another Marine said, gesturing to the damaged plane behind him.

Teddy gave a crooked grin. "Yeah, that would be a great idea."

They helped him remove the film cartridge from the wing-mounted gun camera. He pocketed it carefully. "I'll take this back to the Enterprise myself."

The Marines quickly refueled the extra Wildcat from emergency drums and gave it one last look-over. Despite the dust and tropical wear, it was in perfect flying condition—almost eerie, given the ghost story attached to it.

Teddy climbed into the spare Wildcat, familiarizing himself with the controls. The seat was dry, the instruments clean. It was as if it had been waiting.

He gave a final wave to the Marines.

"Thanks for the bird—and the rescue," he said.

"Anytime, flyboy," the corporal called back. "And do us a favor—find out what happened to the guy who left that plane behind."

Teddy fired up the engine. It caught immediately, the prop spinning into a confident hum. He taxied to the edge of the strip, turned into the wind, and throttled forward.

Moments later, the Wildcat roared into the sky, rising over the reef and into the golden light, with a mystery in his wake—and evidence of two kills tucked in his flight jacket.

The Blue Star and Gold Star tradition began in World War I, when Army Captain Robert L. Queisser created a simple flag to honor his two sons in service. Its design—a white field with a red border and a blue star for each family member in uniform—spread quickly across the country and was soon recognized as an emblem of pride and shared sacrifice. By the war's end, thousands of American homes displayed Blue Star Service Flags in their windows.

As losses mounted, families who endured the death of a loved one replaced a blue star with a gold one. In 1918, President Woodrow Wilson formally acknowledged the Gold Star as a national symbol of honor, a way for the country to recognize families who had paid the highest price. By World War II, the tradition was fully established: Blue Star and Gold Star service flags, lapel pins, and mothers' organizations became a visible reminder of both the nation's courage and the quiet grief carried inside its homes.

ROTATING HOME

Teddy could hardly get off the flight deck. He felt black and blue from all the back-slapping. Sailors lined the catwalks and tower levels like it was a parade, leaning over the rails, shouting his name.

"Davidson bring us a souvenir?"

"Get that man a drink!"

"Hey Wildcat thief!"

What thrilled them most wasn't just that Lieutenant Theodore "Teddy" Davidson had returned — it was that he'd come back in an airplane that wasn't the one he'd taken out.

He had left in his familiar, scarred Wildcat. He had come back in a different Wildcat altogether.

Even the flight commander made a rare trip down to the deck, arms folded, trying and failing not to grin. "I know your Wildcat was pretty beat up," he shouted over the noise, "but did you really have to trade it in on a new one?"

The line set off a wave of laughter up and down the deck. Teddy gave a modest salute and tried to play it off. Truth was, he felt shaky. Grateful. Lucky. He was alive, unhurt, and standing on the carrier instead of floating in a raft or bleeding out in the jungle. That alone felt like a miracle.

But there was a weight on him.

His wingman.

They'd gotten separated during the chaos. The last Teddy had seen of him was a smoking trail and a splash.

Inside the ready room the celebration kept going. Sweat, coffee, hydraulic fluid, cigarette smoke, and adrenaline — the layered smell of combat flying. Pilots crowded around him, hungry for details, and the deck crew squeezed in at the door. Teddy walked them through what had happened, where he'd seen ground fire, how the enemy planes moved, what altitude had been safest, what angles had actually worked.

They laughed in the right places. They whooped when he described setting down in the borrowed Wildcat "like I owned her."

But his mind wasn't done counting heads.

"All right, listen up," the Flight Operations boss said from the doorway. Conversation dropped. He had a folded sheet of message paper in his hand, the kind that came straight off radio traffic.

Teddy straightened, bracing.

"Davidson," the boss said, then to the room, louder: "For those of you who can't keep quiet for five seconds — I have news on Ensign Fuller."

Fuller. Teddy's wingman.

You could feel the room tighten. Somebody muttered, "Come on..."

The Commander glanced down at the sheet. "Recovered by destroyer. Picked up alive. Minor burns, busted ankle. He's on a tin can headed back to base medical. He's going to make it."

The sound that went up wasn't a cheer at first. It was an exhale. A full, rolling release, like the ship itself relaxed a few degrees. Then the cheers came, louder, grateful, almost feral. Someone slapped Teddy on the back hard enough to stagger him into a chair.

Teddy swallowed and scrubbed a hand over his face. He hadn't realized until that moment how much tension had been sitting in his chest like a stone. He let himself grin, a real grin. Fuller was alive. Fuller was okay.

"Hey Davidson," one of the deckhands grinned, "now you can stop moping and act heroic again."

"Yeah," Teddy shot back, "well I'm going to need a clean flight suit first."

That earned him another round of laughter.

A young sailor with nervous posture slipped into the

room, eyes wide like he'd walked into the lion cage at the circus. "Lieutenant Davidson?"

"That's me," Teddy said.

The sailor held out a sealed envelope. Actual paper. Official as a funeral.

Behind him stood the Flight Ops Commander, now with a different expression on his face.

"Teddy," the Commander said, clapping his shoulder, "looks like you're being rotated home."

For a second, the words didn't land.

"Really?" Teddy blinked. "Now?"

"Yes, sir," the boss said. "The Navy has decided you are too valuable to keep in harm's way. You've got travel instructions and orders in that packet. You'll transfer off tomorrow with the next hop for Pearl Harbor. Then you're headed stateside."

There was a low murmur in the room. Some envy. Some pride. Some relief on his behalf.

And in Teddy, a hit of something he hadn't prepared for: disorientation.

The war wasn't over. Not for the squadron. Not for the ship. Certainly not for the Pacific.

But it sounded like, at least for now, his chapter out here was closing.

The rest of the day was quiet work wrapped in noisy goodbye.

He found his crew chief — the man who had coaxed life out of that battered Wildcat time and time again, sometimes with literal wire and prayer. Teddy started to offer a handshake. The chief ignored it and hauled him straight into a hug instead, long and wordless. That hit harder than anything anyone had said.

"Don't let 'em make you pretty back home," the chief muttered finally. "You ain't pretty."

Teddy snorted. "I'll do my best."

He met with the other pilots, gave them what he could — little tactical notes, "watch for that flak pocket here," "don't chase too low," "don't get heroic when you're angry." He named his replacement in the section. He didn't say "don't die." He didn't have to.

That night he didn't sleep much.

By the next morning, he was back in the air — only this time not behind the stick. He rode a transport out, belly full of engine vibration and fuel fumes, bound for Pearl Harbor. He watched the carrier shrink in the distance through the tiny round window and felt, for the first time in months, physically separate from the war.

The ride to Pearl was quiet. Too quiet. Pride, yes. Relief, yes. But also, something tight and sore, like leaving teammates on the field before the game is done.

At Pearl, orders were waiting. The envelope from the ready room wasn't just "go home and rest."

It was an itinerary.

San Francisco.

He stepped off a Navy transport in California and got handed his next set of instructions so fast it made him laugh.

Technically, his assignment back in the States was "public liaison and technical consultant." What that meant in practice was two tracks running side by side.

Track one: he was going to be a face of the war.

War bond rallies. Stages. Civic auditoriums. Newspaper photos. The handsome young naval aviator who'd mixed it up with the enemy and made it back. The story they loved: the boy from Kansas who had gone out to sea and come home a fighter ace-in-the-making.

Track two: he'd been selected to support the Navy's evaluation of a new fighter aircraft — the Chance Vought F4U Corsair. A monster of a machine: bent gull wings, huge propeller, 18-cylinder Pratt & Whitney R-2800 radial engine throwing over 2,000 horsepower, better than 400 miles per hour in level flight, faster than anything the Japanese were flying head-on. The Navy believed this airplane could win the war from the air. But it had problems coming aboard a carrier. Bad ones.

Carrier landings were chewing it up. The long nose blocked forward view in final approach. The landing bounce could get violent. Yaw on touchdown could throw a pilot sideways so fast he'd hook a wing, and then it got ugly. The Marines loved the Corsair off land runways. The Navy still wasn't convinced it was safe at sea.

They wanted combat pilots — people who had actually flown in anger, who understood what panic felt like at 200 miles per hour — to help bridge the gap between the engineers on paper and the steel on the deck.

That was Teddy now.

But before he could touch a Corsair, he had to hit the circuit.

The orders spelled it out in neat Navy type:

— San Francisco: Civic bond drive, photographs with local officials, interviews.

— Denver: War bond rally, Veterans of Foreign Wars banquet appearance, luncheon with plant workers.

— Wichita: Aircraft workers' rally, meet-and-greet at the train station, high school gym speech.

— Stratford, Connecticut: Chance Vought / Vought-Sikorsky plant visit, technical review with engineering and test staff, one-week embedded evaluation.

— Norfolk Naval Air Station: three-day familiarization and briefing cycle.

— Then Pensacola: extended assignment with flight training command to work with front-line pilots on Corsair approach and landing procedures.

It was a map of America stitched together by rail lines and hotel rooms.

He read through it and smiled despite himself.

Caroline.

Right away he wired her.

CAROLINE STOP ORDERS IN HAND STOP SAN FRANCISCO DENVER WICHITA STRATFORD CONNECTICUT NORFOLK THEN PENSACOLA STOP TELL ME WHERE YOU ARE STOP TELL ME WHERE TO FIND YOU STOP I'M COMING HOME STOP

He sent it before he'd even found a clean uniform.

Her answer came back fast.

TEDDY STOP I WILL BE THERE IF HUMANLY POSSIBLE STOP I AM SO PROUD OF YOU STOP DO NOT CRASH ANY TRAINS OR AIRPLANES BEFORE I GET TO YOU STOP CAROLINE STOP

It made him laugh out loud.

But "if humanly possible" was doing a lot of work.

As the war progressed, it became clear to military leaders that rotating front-line personnel—especially pilots—was both strategically wise and morally necessary. The relentless strain of aerial combat could wear down even the strongest minds and bodies. If left unchecked, that stress could lead to fatal errors and the loss of highly trained individuals.

Bringing experienced pilots home served several purposes. Not only did it preserve their lives, but it also allowed the military to capitalize on their knowledge. These veterans became flight instructors, training the next generation of combat aviators. Others took roles leading training schools, advising aircraft manufacturers on combat-tested improvements, or speaking to civilian audiences on bond drives, helping to finance the war effort. These men, once symbols of frontline heroism, became vital links in sustaining and winning the war on the home front.

AT LONG LAST

San Francisco was loud.

They put him in dress whites and pinned him with more ribbons than he was comfortable wearing. He stood on a municipal stage under a banner that read BUY WAR BONDS: BRING THEM HOME SOONER. The mayor introduced him like a movie star. The crowd — families, shipyard workers on lunch break, little kids waving paper flags — leaned forward, hungry.

He hadn't rehearsed what to say. He didn't like rehearsed.

He told them the truth.

"I don't think of myself as a hero," he started, and it got quiet. "Where I just came from, the heroes are the kids on the deck crew who run out under live props and hot engines to get us ready and then haul us back in one piece. They're the mechanics patching bullet holes with tape so we can go again. They're the corpsmen who can stitch a man closed on a table that's bolted to a steel floor that's still moving. I'm just the one who gets the attention because you can see the airplane."

That line made them laugh. It also made them love him.

He talked about Ensign Fuller — "My wingman is alive because a destroyer turned toward fire to pick him up. They did not have to do that. They did it anyway." — and you could feel the room swell with pride that they were part of a country that behaved like that.

He painted pictures: what it felt like to dive, what a twenty-millimeter cannon flash looked like in sunlight, what it sounded like when flak burst too close and your whole plane rang like a bell. He let them into it. He made it real.

And then he did the job.

"We are winning because we are outworking them," he said. "Every dollar you put into those bonds turns into steel, turns into fuel, turns into planes, and turns into us getting home. You don't just get to say you support the war. You get to prove it."

By the time he walked offstage, they were already shouting where to buy.

Afterward, reporters shoved microphones and flash-bulbs at him. He answered what he could. He smiled the polite smile they all wanted. He shook hands until his fingers hurt.

Then, alone for five blessed minutes, he found a phone.

The operator actually had to route the call through a Navy line to get her. She was that hard to catch.

"Caroline McKenna— hold for Lieutenant Davidson— hold please—"

Then her voice.

"Teddy?"

He closed his eyes. Just hearing her almost buckled him.

"Caroline."

"Oh my God." She laughed, and there was relief in it and tension too. "Tell me where you are."

"San Francisco," he said. "Next is Denver. Then Wichita. Then Stratford, Connecticut, for a week in some airplane factory. Then Norfolk. Then Pensacola, where they claim they're going to let me boss test pilots around."

"I'm shuttling between Pensacola and Jacksonville this week," she said. "They've got me flying personnel and instruments back and forth and sitting in on briefings I'm not supposed to be in. Next week I'm in Pensacola all week. The week after that they're sending me to New Orleans for procurement meetings, and then possibly back to Pensacola but only for two days before a courier run up the coast."

"So," he said softly, "that's a no on dinner in Denver."

She made a pained sound. "I hate this."

"Me too."

They sat in the quiet of that unfixable thing. The connection crackled.

"I'll get to you," he said.

"You'd better," she said, and then softer, "Don't let them pin you to a podium forever. I need you in one piece."

He smiled. "Yes, ma'am."

The line clicked dead. He stood there a long time, receiver still in his hand.

Denver was different.

Instead of a civic plaza, it was an indoor rally in a VFW hall that smelled like coffee, wool uniforms, and cigar smoke. They sat him at a head table next to a one-armed Marine and a mother with a gold star pin on her lapel. Her son had gone down somewhere off Guadalcanal and never come back.

When Teddy stood to talk, he changed it.

He didn't lead with airplanes.

He led with the mother.

"We talk about victory like it's a flag," he said, voice steady, hand resting lightly on the table in front of the woman. "But sometimes victory is just making sure her boy mattered."

Silence. Total.

He talked about why they fight — not just tactics, not just ships, but what it means to keep people like her from losing another son. He didn't even mention bonds until the end.

Denver loved him for that.

He slept on the train that night, uniform jacket folded under his head, hat over his eyes, boots braced against his duffel so nobody walked off with it. The rails hummed under him like a lullaby and a threat.

The next stop was his, though not officially on the schedule.

Wichita.

The war had turned Wichita into a foundry with a skyline. Every block either built something, fixed something, or fed someone who did.

He stepped off the train and the first thing that hit him was the smell of oil and hot metal. The second was how familiar the air felt. Kansas air. Dry, honest, a little dusty. Home.

They had arranged a rally at the train station itself — portable PA system, bunting, school band in uniforms that didn't quite fit the kids wearing them. Reporters. Wives in summer dresses. Men with their sleeves rolled. Factory badges everywhere.

He gave them the fighter pilot show this time — fast, loud, punchy. They laughed, they cheered, they pushed in for handshakes and signatures. Some of the young mechanics looked at him like he was what they wanted to be next year.

Then, finally, finally, he got a sliver of something for himself.

"Lieutenant Davidson?" a Navy liaison lieutenant (who looked all of nineteen) said. "You've got forty-eight hours of family leave authorized while we refit your rail orders."

Forty-eight hours.

Two days.

Livingston, Kansas.

Home.

His parents' house hadn't changed in any structural way — same porch, same steps, same wind chimes made out of scrap copper his father swore sounded like "good weather bells." But it felt smaller when he walked through the gate. Or maybe he just felt bigger.

His mother saw him first. She didn't run; she launched. Arms around his neck, face buried in his shoulder, sobbing while she laughed and scolded him at the same time.

"I told God, I said, 'You bring my boy home,' and now look at you," she said, pushing back just to hold his face in both her hands. "You're too thin. You're handsome as sin, but you're too thin."

"I'm eating," he protested, grinning. "The Navy feeds us. I promise."

His father didn't make a scene. He just stood there in the doorway for a long second, jaw clenched, eyes wet, then stepped forward and wrapped Teddy in a hug that said all the things he didn't.

When they finally let him sit, his mother started cooking like she was fueling an army. Eggs, biscuits, steak, potatoes, coffee, more eggs. Teddy tried to help. She smacked his hand away with a wooden spoon.

That night, after his mother went to bed, Teddy sat

at the kitchen table with his father. Two coffee cups. The only light the dull yellow over the sink.

"So," his father said. "They done with you?"

Teddy shook his head. "Not even close."

His father grunted. "Figured."

"They're sending me around to talk people into buying bonds," Teddy said, rolling the coffee cup between his hands. "Then they're putting me into this Corsair program. New fighter. Fastest thing we've got. Strong as a farm gate. Mean. But it's trying to kill people on landing. They want me to help figure out how not to let that happen."

His father looked at him, and Teddy saw the pride but also a flicker of worry.

"That sound safer than what you've been doing," his father said.

Teddy smiled faintly. "Define 'safer.'"

They both laughed.

Before he went up to his old room — still the same bed, still the same pennant on the wall, still the same squeak in the floorboard by the closet — he wrote again to Caroline.

CAROLINE STOP HOME TWO NIGHTS ONLY STOP MOTHER FEEDING ME LIKE I HAVEN'T EATEN IN YEARS STOP I MISS YOU STOP WISH YOU WERE HERE AT THIS TABLE WITH ME STOP CAN YOU MEET ME IN PENSACOLA WHEN I LAND STOP I WILL FIND YOU STOP TEDDY STOP

He stared at that last line, then underlined "I WILL FIND YOU."

From Kansas he caught the eastbound line.

Past fields. Past towns with blackout curtains in the windows and little flags in front yards, some with blue stars, some with gold. Past soldiers asleep sitting up. Past sailors with duffels for pillows. Past women in factory coveralls, grease still under their fingernails, dead asleep against the train glass.

The war had pulled the whole country into motion. You could feel it in every car, every station platform. America wasn't watching this war. America was in it.

He rode coach, not sleeper. He didn't ask for special treatment. He didn't want it.

He practiced, in his head, how he'd say it.

He could see it — her face, the way her laugh always started in her throat and then spilled out like she'd just surprised herself with joy. He could see the way she'd stood on that train platform back when he shipped out. He could hear what she'd said. Again, a kiss goodbye.

He couldn't shake the idea that "soon" owed them.

Stratford, Connecticut looked nothing like Kansas and nothing like the Pacific. It looked like America hammered into war steel.

The Vought-Sikorsky plant sat on the Housatonic River, huge and alive. The place didn't sleep. Rows and rows of half-built Corsairs sat in lines under high windows, their bare wings arched like gulls frozen in mid-dive. Sparks lit and died. Rivet guns snapped in staccato bursts. Women in coveralls leaned into the work with the same intensity as any front-line pilot.

They gave Teddy a hard hat and a visitor badge and

then, very quickly, they stopped treating him like a celebrity and started treating him like a data source.

They walked him through the assembly line. He stood next to a bare Corsair airframe, skin off, guts exposed, and he ran his fingertips along the massive Pratt & Whitney R-2800 radial, that 18-cylinder furnace that could throw more than 2,000 horses forward and tear the sky. He'd flown against Zeros. He knew what it meant to have not just speed but climb and dive authority. On paper, this thing outclassed almost anything the Japanese had.

If they could just get it safely on and off a carrier.

He watched carrier-simulation tests in the back lot. They had painted a "deck" outline on asphalt and built a mock island and LSO platform. Pilots came in on approach, noses high, wings twitching. Some were beautiful. Some were ugly. One came in, hit hard, bounced left, and you could see the whole airplane try to yaw itself into a cartwheel.

"There," Teddy said, pointing. "Freeze it right there. Did you see that skip? He's correcting on instinct, but his instinct is wrong because he's blind over that nose. You've got to train them to crab sooner with right rudder before they flare."

The engineers scribbled.

He stayed a week.

He ate in the same cafeteria line as line workers. He sat in meetings until midnight. He crawled up onto a Corsair's wing root and leaned into the cockpit, studying the sight picture, imagining the last five seconds before wheels hit steel.

At night, exhausted in a little Army-issue cot in a borrowed office, he wrote to Caroline again.

CAROLINE STOP STRATFORD CONNECTICUT STOP I AM SITTING INSIDE THE BELLY OF THE PLANE THEY WANT ME TO TAME STOP IT IS A BEAST AND IT WANTS TO KILL ANYONE WHO DOES NOT RESPECT IT STOP I THINK I CAN HELP STOP I THINK THIS IS MY WORK NOW STOP PLEASE TELL ME YOU WILL BE IN PENSACOLA STOP I AM COUNTING HOURS STOP TEDDY STOP

Her reply, a day later:

TEDDY STOP I WILL INTERCEPT YOU IN PENSACOLA STOP I SWEAR IT STOP I'M ON TEMPORARY DUTY THERE NEXT WEEK STOP DO NOT LET ANY ADMIRAL REASSIGN YOU UNTIL I GET THERE STOP CAROLINE STOP

He laughed out loud when he read that. Then he pressed the paper to his lips and just stayed there, breathing her words.

Norfolk Naval Air Station.

Three days.

Norfolk wasn't about speeches and it wasn't about theory. Norfolk was about urgency.

Teddy had barely stepped down from the train when a compact officer in a flight jacket intercepted him on the platform. The man was already walking, already talking.

"Lieutenant Davidson?" he said. "Lieutenant Commander Webster. Flight instruction. We're behind schedule."

He didn't wait for a reply.

They climbed into a staff car that never quite stopped rolling, and Webster began talking the way experienced instructors do when time matters—fast, precise, and stripped of anything ornamental.

"You've read the Corsair packet," Webster said.

"Yes, sir."

"Good. Forget half of it. The airplane doesn't care what you've read. She cares what you do. You've landed fighters under pressure. You've dealt with torque. That helps. What you haven't done is land this."

They broke onto the flight line, and Teddy saw it immediately.

A single Corsair sat forward of the line, engine already warmed, propeller biting the air with slow, confident authority. The dark-blue fuselage looked coiled and impatient, like something being held back by courtesy alone. Crewmen waited nearby. Chocks in place. Oil glinting along the cowling seams.

Webster glanced at his watch. "We'll talk when you're back."

There was no ceremony. No speeches.

Preflight was brisk and exacting. Teddy moved around the aircraft alone, hands on metal, eyes sharp, mind already shifting gears. Control surfaces free. Fuel secure. Oil pressure steady. Magnetos checked. The massive Pratt & Whitney radial pulsed with restrained violence.

Webster stood a few yards away, watching everything.

"Taxi when ready," he called.

Teddy eased the Corsair forward and immediately felt the weight of it—the way the airplane wanted to wander if you relaxed for even a moment. This wasn't a Wildcat. This was power concentrated forward, demanding constant respect.

At the runway, he paused.

"Don't baby it," Webster called. "Fly it."

Teddy advanced the throttle.

The response was immediate and brutal in the best possible way. Acceleration slammed him back in the seat. Torque came alive under his feet. He fed in right rudder, held it there, and the Corsair surged forward as if it had been waiting all morning for permission.

The nose lifted.

The ground fell away.

The climb was astonishing.

"Jesus," Teddy muttered to himself, grinning despite the tension.

He stayed in the pattern.

The runway ahead was painted with a full carrier outline—island, deck edges, touchdown zone—everything but the sea. Teddy flew it like it mattered. Nose high. Forward visibility nearly gone. Peripheral cues only.

Approach.

Power.

Rudder.

Correction.

Landing.

The Corsair hit harder than a Wildcat and tried to skip if he let it. Teddy didn't. He held her down, power steady, attitude firm, then shoved the throttle forward again and let the engine haul him back into the sky.

Again.

And again.

Webster watched from the edge of the field, tracking each pass with binoculars, occasionally speaking into a handheld radio. No instructions. Just timing calls. Just presence.

By the tenth landing, Teddy's shirt was soaked.

By the fifteenth, his corrections came earlier.

By the twentieth, the airplane stopped arguing with him.

When he finally taxied clear and shut down, his hands were steady and his heart was pounding the way it only did after something honest.

Webster was waiting when he climbed down.

"Now," the lieutenant commander said evenly, "Now you're allowed to talk about the Corsair."

Only then did they walk toward the briefing room.

They threw him in a room with test pilots, flight instructors, and a commander who had "CARRIER QUALIFIED" practically stamped on his forehead.

"All right, Davidson," the commander said, "you've actually been shot at. We've got a plane that'll win the war if it stops trying to snap pilots' necks on landing. Tell us where the stupid is."

Teddy didn't bother with rank politeness. They didn't need polite. They needed honest.

"The stupid," he said, "is expecting a twenty-two-year-old with six hours in type to improvise his way through a blind, nose-high, high-torque, high-bounce landing on a moving postage stamp while scared. The plane is not forgiving enough for improvisation. You have to make the last thirty seconds procedural, not instinct."

They stared at him. Then they all started talking at once.

For three days they picked every angle. He ran mock approaches. He sat in on training briefs. He worked with landing signal officers on timing their paddles so the pilot felt guided instead of yelled at. He advocated for raising the pilot's seat and tweaking the gear oleos to kill some of the bounce on contact — changes already being discussed at Vought in Stratford, which made the engineers in Connecticut and the trainers in Virginia feel, for once, like the same team instead of two different wars.

He slept badly, dreamed hard, woke early.

And on the morning of the fourth day, he reported to transport.

Destination: Pensacola Naval Air Station.

As his transport descended toward Pensacola, Teddy leaned to the oval window and watched Florida slide into view. The Gulf water flashed bright. The sun cut hard lines of shadow off the hangars and control towers. He could make out trainers taxiing below like fat dragonflies. Rows of F6F Hellcats sat out on the apron. And then — there. Corsairs. Broad, bent wings like a bird of prey's shoulders. Dark blue skins throwing back the light like oil.

His heart kicked.

This was it.

He pressed his forehead lightly to the glass and exhaled.

Please be there. Please be there. Please be there.

The wheels kissed runway. The engines wound down. The cabin filled with heat and the smell of hot metal.

He grabbed his B-4 bag and stepped down into Florida air.

It hit him like a wall — heat, humidity, sound. There were people everywhere along the chain-link fence: uniforms, cadets, officers' wives, ground crew in grease-stained shirts, even a few kids from town who'd somehow slipped onto the field. Word travels when a pilot from the shooting war is inbound.

He scanned the crowd without meaning to. It wasn't conscious. It was hunger.

The shouting faded. The buzz of the airfield dropped into the background. It all narrowed.

Then he saw her.

Caroline.

Dark hair neatly tucked under her cover, uniform pressed, chin high. She wasn't smiling yet. She was moving. Focused. Cutting straight toward him like a torpedo in heels.

The B-4 bag hit the tarmac at his feet. She dropped her orders. They collided in the middle of the arrivals area, arms around each other, and for a moment the whole world just...stopped.

Every mile. Every letter. Every crackling phone call. Every almost.

Gone.

It was just her in his arms, breathing fast, her face pressed to his neck, his hands in her hair, both of them shaking.

He pulled back only enough to look at her. Eyes glossy. Cheeks flushed. Trying to smile and cry at the same time.

Before she could say a word, he dropped to one knee.

The gasp from the fence line rippled like a breeze.

He reached into his pocket and pulled out the little black box he'd carried since Wichita. He hadn't been able to send it in a letter. He hadn't dared say the words on a phone line. This had to be here. In front of her.

"Caroline," he said, and suddenly his voice wasn't as steady as he'd planned. "I didn't want to ask you until I was sure I'd come back. But now — now I'm home."

Her hand flew to her mouth. Tears actually spilled this time.

"You don't have to say anything if you don't want to," he rushed, and it was almost funny, because he was the one who'd stared down cannon fire and now he was nervous. "I just — I can't go one more mile without you. I can't go one more day not knowing you're mine. Will you—"

She let out a short, incredulous laugh and shook her head at him, wiping tears with the heel of her hand. "You idiot," she said, voice breaking into a grin. "I was hoping you'd ask the moment you stepped off the plane."

She didn't even wait for him to stand. She threw her arms around him and practically tackled him, whispering into his ear, "Yes. Yes. Yes."

The crowd around them erupted. Sailors whistled. Aviators applauded like he'd just stuck the perfect carrier landing. Somebody yelled, "Buy that girl a ring, Lieutenant!" and set off another round of laughter and cheers.

Overhead, as if on cue, a single dark-blue Corsair rolled gracefully over the field, banking in a lazy arc, sun sliding along the bent gull of its wings. It looked like a predator at rest.

Teddy held her and closed his eyes.

Their war — the one fought against time and distance and orders and train schedules — was finally over.

And this time, there would be no kiss goodbye.

EPILOGUE

World War II was the most consequential conflict in human history, reshaping global politics, technology, economics, and international society. Its effects extended far beyond the battlefield, altering the balance of power, sparking unprecedented innovation, and fostering global trade and interdependence. The aftermath of 1939–1945 continues to influence the twenty-first century.

Politically, the war dismantled European empires and elevated the United States and Soviet Union as superpowers. Devastated Europe created a power vacuum that ushered in a bipolar world order—the Cold War—dominating international relations for decades. The war also accelerated decolonization, as weakened European powers faced demands for independence in Asia and Africa, leading to a proliferation of sovereign states.

Japan underwent one of the era's most remarkable transformations. Defeated and devastated by atomic bombs, it was reshaped under U.S.-led occupation directed by General Douglas MacArthur. The 1947 constitution established democracy, civil rights, and pacifism, while reforms in land distribution, labor rights, and education laid the groundwork for a modern society. Japan's shift from militarist empire to democratically exemplifies profound postwar political change.

New institutions reflected the drive for cooperation: the United Nations (1945) aimed to prevent future wars, while the Bretton Woods Conference (1944) created the International Monetary Fund and World Bank to coordinate global economics.

The war drove rapid innovation. In medicine, mass-produced penicillin and advances in surgery, blood transfusion, and rehabilitation saved millions and shaped postwar health systems. Armaments evolved with ballistic missiles (like the German V-2), automatic weapons, and improved tanks. Aviation leaped from biplanes to jets (e.g., Me 262 and Gloster Meteor) and long-range bombers (B-29), enabling postwar commercial flight, with radar transforming navigation and defense.

Most momentous was the Manhattan Project, birthing nuclear weapons used on Hiroshima and Nagasaki, ushering in an era of unparalleled destructive power and influencing international relations ever since. Other advances—in computing (Colossus, ENIAC), logistics, and materials (plastics, synthetic rubber)—rippled into civilian life.

Economically, the war mobilized resources on an immense scale. In the United States, government spending ended the Great Depression, achieved full employment, and expanded industry, while women's workforce participation spurred social change. The Marshall Plan (1948–1952) provided over $12 billion in aid (equivalent to ~$150 billion today) to rebuild Western Europe, creating markets for U.S. goods, containing communism, and promoting globalization.

Japan's recovery, supported by U.S. guidance, emphasized education, land reform, and industrial focus, propelling it to leadership in electronics and automobiles. Germany similarly rebuilt with aid, integrating into the European economy. The U.S. dollar became the global reserve currency under Bretton Woods, fostering trade stability. Initiatives like GATT (1947) reduced barriers, laying foundations for free trade zones and the European Economic Community.

This era marked the end of economic isolation, tying prosperity to international exchange despite Cold War divisions.

The war's human dimension—total mobilization, shared sacrifices, and blurred civilian-military lines—reinforced the need for ongoing cooperation in peace.

World War II's lasting legacy lies in the world it forged: the fall of empires and rise of a bipolar order; the nuclear and technological revolutions; America's economic dominance alongside Europe's and Asia's recovery through aid and trade; and an interdependent global system that persists today. Japan's rebirth symbolizes this paradox—devastation yielding renewal, defeat fostering freedom and enduring partnership.

When we explore personal stories amid this vast

conflict—as *Again, A Kiss Goodbye* does—we see how individuals, through love, loss, courage, and resilience, lived and shaped these monumental changes. History is written not only in treaties and technologies, but in human perseverance.